A Part of Her, Too

P.A. Spence

Caliche Roads Press

Corpus Christi, Texas

First Printing: August 2023 by P.A. Spence
Second Printing: September 2023 by P.A. Spence
ISBN: 978-1-7362584-7-7   (pbk)
ISBN: 978-1-7362584-8-4   (ebook)
LCCN: 2023915311
P.A. Spence
www.calicheroadspress.webador.com

For you, Jerry, and the love and strength you share as you walk beside me through all our challenges.

Our faith can move mountains. Matthew 17:20

Author's Note

I humbly thank God for helping me share this story that is all too true for too many. My heartfelt thanks go out to David E. Spence, for helping me set the story on course. A special thanks goes to Candace Wofford, for giving me her time and guidance. Many thanks go to Jennifer Pshigoda, for giving up her time to pour through this work and offer her professional advice.

Table of Contents

Chapter 1

The Punch

The last of the fall moths found their way up to a second-floor bedroom window of the Delta Phi fraternity house. The soft rhythmic tapping of their heads against the pane as they tried to reach the glow of the ceiling light broke the silence in the room.

Annie's closed eyes fluttered as she struggled to open them. Light seeped through the dark lashes of her right eye, and like a window blind tightly pulled and released, her right lid shot open as her left remained heavily shut. Above her hung a bright bare lightbulb with the word

Sylvania printed in an arch across it. For a moment she didn't recognize her surroundings. She heard music and the words, "Roxanne, you don't have to put on the red light" and recognized The Police playing on a radio or record player; she wasn't sure. A groggy thickness moved slowly through her thoughts as she tried to open both eyes to get a sense of where she was. Her body was held down by an invisible weight, and her muscles felt weak, making it hard to breathe and move. She arched her brows, and her left eyelid rolled open. She briefly stared up at the light fixture one last time before her eyes quickly slammed shut. Annie fell back into a dreamless sleep, and all her thoughts were snuffed out.

***

He glanced up at the light fixture and wondered if he should turn off the switch. One light bulb, with its off-white glow, flickered. Rubbing his chin stubble with the back of his hand, he turned his gaze to her and watched her sleep. Her long dark hair spread across his bed, like the black flames of a raging campfire. Her skin, tanned from a summer of tennis-court sun, was smooth and flawless. Her petite body displayed the curvature of an hourglass figure and toned muscles. She was beautiful.

He reached for his Pentax camera on his desk and captured the moment on black and white film. These were the last few shots on his film roll, and he knew that using the university photography program's darkroom wouldn't be an issue.

He admired her for a moment longer. She looked so peaceful, a Spanish doll sleeping in his bed. She was a prize that any guy could have taken, but she was his. He believed she was the one for him. As his dreamy thoughts filtered through his head a twitch of a finger on her left hand showed that she was awakening, and his dreams were squashed. A panic button deep in his chest sent an alert signal to his thoughts to prepare a protective shield for himself.

He really didn't mean to take it so far. They had only kissed once in the three months that they were dating, and now she lay at an angle on his bed, dress hiked up to her waist, right leg hanging off the edge, and pink panties and nylon hose twisted around her ankle. He leaned over her and removed her hosiery from her small dangling foot and threw them in the plastic wastebasket by the door. While pulling up her panties, he noticed dime-sized red spots spreading and growing into a quarter-sized stain on his gray bed sheets. He grabbed his yellow bath towel from a nail on the wall and covered the scarlet symbol of innocence lost. Smoothing out her blue taffeta dress, he worked quickly as he tried to rearrange the setting to appear as if nothing had happened.

He didn't have a plan for this. He hadn't considered the possibility that she was a virgin, but the evidence was undeniable. She wasn't a drinker and had declined beer or liquor, so he had only given her half a roofie dissolved in her punch. He didn't give her the Wapatui punch others were drinking because he had heard it had been laced with quaaludes. His idea was to have fun with her, to show her a good time, but she needed to relax. He had used this method with Tanya, his last girlfriend, and it worked well; but this dose for Annie seemed to work differently. The effects kicked in within thirty minutes, and two hours later, she was still passed out. It was now nearing two in the morning, but the party at the Delta Phi fraternity house was pounding and reverberating off the walls. He chewed on the inside of his right cheek as he tried to come up with an explanation.

He needed a defense. She was going to know what happened, and he was going to deny there was any drug involved. He'd just say that she wanted it, and she begged him to have sex with her. He would make her believe it. He had convinced her of other things before even though she knew the truth. He found this was a great skill he had. Making people believe they were wrong, convincing them of the opposite of what they believed, was a gift.

As he stood up from his desk chair, the hard plastic caps on the feet scraped across the tile floor, making an ear-piercing sound like fingernails raked down a chalkboard. He immediately regretted this move and placed his hands behind his neck like a man apprehended by the police, his dark wavy locks pressing against his head. *Shit.* He turned to the beautiful girl in his bed and held his breath. A soft moan escaped her lips, and he stood still. The light bulb overhead flickered again.

A brief flash of light stirred her slumber. She opened both eyes, blinking slowly, trying to focus. She could see the brass deadbolts on the door blur in and out of view. Turning her head made her dizzy, but she was able to recognize Johan standing near her, his large dark eyes connecting with hers. Feeling a bit nauseous and cotton-mouthed, she asked, "Where are we?" as she cleared cobwebs in her throat.

"We're in my room. The party's still going strong. Do you want to join everyone?" He stayed standing by the bed, hoping if he just moved the conversation forward, she wouldn't ask any questions. He held his breath.

Annie breathed deeply as a dull cramp in her lower abdomen made its presence known. Between her legs she felt stinging and throbbing, and a sticky substance was hardening on her inner thighs. Fearing that she had just started her period, she slowly sat up and thought she should head back to the dorms. As her vision cleared and the grogginess subsided, she noticed she was no longer wearing her pantyhose or her shoes. She slowly stood up, briefly lost her balance, and woozily looked around for her footwear. One black stiletto was on the floor at the foot of the bed, and the other was by the door. She picked up her shoes and turned to Johan who was standing near the bed, not offering any assistance. "I think I need to leave. I'm not feeling well," Annie said, voice quivering.

He noted the shake in her voice and answered, "Yeah, sure. You want me to walk you back to the dorms?" Wanting to return to the party and avoid any conversation with her, he hoped she would decline the offer. He had missed out on a fun night having to sit with her while she slept.

"No. I just want to find Maddie and Christy," she said. She held her shoes to her chest and embarrassingly walked over to the bolted door, unlocked all three locks, and left the room without looking back.

:: 7 ::

Chapter 2

Unexpected Exit

In the hallway against the wall was a line of fraternity boys. All of them looked intently at her. She wondered if she had stained her dress, and they could see. She staggered forward, straightened up, then wove in and out of groups of drunk partygoers with punch-stained tongues. She spotted Maddie speaking with a fraternity boy as her curly fire-red hair bounced like springing coils every time she moved her head. Leaning into Maddie's ear to speak over The Rolling Stones'

"Beast of Burden," Annie interrupted, "Maddie, can you come with me?"

"Annie? What? What's wrong?" Maddie Alaniz pulled away from the boy and stood in the dim light of the living room. Her five-foot-seven slender frame cast a long shadow on the white wall. Annie, being only five foot four, looked up to Maddie in more ways than one. "What's going on?" Maddie asked.

"I don't know. Something has happened. I think I started my period. I don't know if that's it, but I need to go. I need to go now." She stood barefoot in the living room of the fraternity house, trying to avoid being noticed. "Have you seen Christy?"

"I think she's upstairs with Luis. Should I go get her?" Without waiting for an answer, Maddie left her post on the couch and sprinted up the stairs to the second floor. She worked past obnoxious, drunk fraternity boys, cackling, inebriated girls, and witty, stoned intellectuals all discussing global warming. Christy was in a bedroom with Luis drinking beer and watching television. Out of breath, Maddie said, "Christy. We need to go. Something is wrong with Annie."

***

Having known Maddie for two years, Christy Ruiz recognized her friend's serious tone and didn't hesitate. She grabbed her purse, kissed her boyfriend, Luis Diaz, and followed Maddie to the door. "Luis. I've gotta go. My girl needs me."

"Okay. Do you girls need me to walk you back up to school?" He asked as the creases of concern spread over his brow.

Christy heard his serious tone and said, "No. We've got this. There's safety in numbers, right?" She smiled at him and appreciated his kind, gentle nature, his chocolate brown eyes, and his chiseled jawline. He reminded her of Chip, the sweet and loyal chocolate Labrador she left back home in El Paso. Luis was a year ahead of her in school, and they had been dating for two years. Even though her pre-law schedule and his pre-med plans kept them busy, they managed to make time for each other.

"Right," he assured her. "Call me when you get in."

"Okay." She turned to Maddie and said, "Let's go. Where is she?"

"I left her downstairs in the living room. She's not looking right. She's got her shoes in her hands, and she looks afraid. Something is wrong," Maddie exclaimed and hurried down the stairs; the urgent clopping sounds of her wedged shoes as she descended the wooden steps went unnoticed by the partygoers. The music in the living room blasted tunes from The Doors; the party DJ had an eclectic taste in music. The festivities downstairs continued as drunk students wandered in and out of the smoky room, but Annie was missing. Maddie took Christy's hand and wove around the obnoxious laughter of drunk girls.

At two in the morning, the party seemed like it was never going to end. It was known by all that this fraternity was notorious for having the police called out to break up late gatherings. Nothing good ever happened at a party after 2:00 am. Maddie ushered her out a side door that led to the front yard and spotted Annie standing barefooted at the end of the driveway, searching the sea of partygoers for her friends.

"There she is. Annie, we're coming!" Maddie shouted. The crowd had spilled out into the yard, but no one noticed the three girls leaving. No one even seemed to care. The girls hugged each other, and Maddie asked, "Annie, do you want to put on your shoes?"

"No. I'll be able to get away from this place quicker if I just go barefooted. Can we just go?" Not waiting for an answer, Annie turned and started up the street.

The three girls were not the only ones headed back up the hill to the university. A boy in a light blue polo shirt with University Support Services printed across the back was escorting a giggling group of sorority sisters clad in matching pink tops and black shorts. Several feet behind them was a couple hand-in-hand, meandering through the darkness of the dimly lit street. Annie, Maddie, and Christy walked the three blocks to the university in silence. Austin streets at night could be either dark and scary or lit by pub lights and filled with music. This road from the fraternity house to the university was a neighborhood street, and most porches were dark, lights turned off.

Once on campus, they walked past the yellow-lit clock tower and trekked their way to Jesten Hall. Reaching the building first, Maddie pulled the door open for Christy and Annie to pass. The west-wing community areas were empty, but some students were using the study rooms to finish up projects due on Monday. Maddie pressed the cracked "Up" button of the elevator, and it dinged its arrival. Together they boarded, and the cart squealed and shook as it shuttled the girls to the tenth floor.

The dorm was coed with male students living on one floor of the building and females on the other, yet with so many students living in the same building, the wings were empty. As they entered the quiet hall, Maddie rummaged for her key in her black clutch purse, produced it, and swiftly unlocked the door to the suite they shared. Without hesitation, Annie hurried over to her closet, grabbed her toiletry basket, sweatpants and T-shirt, and a clean pair of underwear. Without speaking a word, she entered the bathroom and locked the door behind her.

Christy stood motionless in the dark room and held her breath as she watched Annie's every move. Once the bathroom lock clicked in its chamber she sighed. "Maddie, what do you think happened?" Christy whispered.

"I don't know. She just walked over to me and said she needed to come home." Maddie slid off her shoes, pulled out a pair of sweatpants and T-shirt from the top drawer of her dresser, and slipped out of her dress. "I'm scared. I've never seen her look like that. She was afraid, really afraid. Her eyes were wide and glassy; I've never seen her like that," she repeated. She kicked her wedges aside.

Christy stepped over Maddie's shoes and sat on the edge of her own bed. "I'm going to stay dressed in case Annie needs me to take her somewhere." Leaning over to her nightstand, she pulled a hair scrunchie out of the top drawer, gathered her dark, wavy hair, and rolled it up into a messy bun. Her eyes darted around the room then looked back at the bathroom door.

The dorm room was set up with three beds assigned to a wall with the fourth wall housing the entrance door. Maddie's bed shared the wall with the bathroom door. She sat on her hands on the edge of her bed across from Christy and bit her lower lip as she watched her roommate. After what seemed like an eternity of silence, she finally spoke, "What do you think we should do?"

Christy looked at Maddie for a moment then said, "We wait. Annie hasn't told us anything. Maybe something just spooked her. Hey, have you seen my car keys?" She was now standing at her desk scouring for her keys.

Maddie removed one hand from under her thigh and pointed to Christy's backpack hanging on the bedpost.

"Did you check your backpack? Sometimes you put them in there."

Christy gave her a quirky smile and said, "Of course!"

In the bathroom, Annie inspected her clothes. There was no blood on her dress nor on her panties. She didn't know what had happened to her hosiery. She took the mirror from her basket and placed it between her knees. Dried blood was stuck to the sides of her thighs, but there was no fresh blood. Although she tended to be irregular, it didn't make sense that her flow wasn't heavy.

She started the shower and waited for it to get to the right temperature before stepping in. As the water ran down her body, she first gently soaped up then her cleansing became more vigorous as a need to scrub every part of herself overtook her. The stinging and rawness she felt between her legs frightened her, and soap made it worse.

She leaned against the wall with her eyes closed, trying to remember what happened at the party. Her mind raced, searching every crevice of her memory, but there was nothing. Everything was blank. Yet, her body was speaking to her, telling her that something had happened. She slid to the floor and hugged her knees. Breathing heavily and rocking her body, she tried to soothe herself as strong, unfamiliar feelings grew first in her abdomen, moved to her throat, and clung to her thoughts. An abstract picture in reds, blues, and blacks formed in her mind, and she felt as if her breath had been punched out of her. She had a sense of knowing yet not knowing what had happened at the party down the street.

With knees pulled up to her chest, she sat on the white tile under the hot spray of the showerhead for fifteen minutes. Something ugly in her was growing. It grabbed her by the throat and choked her. It pulled at her and knotted up in her stomach; she was starting to hate herself. "It's all my fault. I shouldn't have gone to that party. I put myself in that situation." Without warning, disgust and shame grew like twins in her mind and were born right there on the bathroom floor.

Chapter 3

Fraternal Order

The Delta Phi house was rocking. Loud music was blaring, and a group of fraternity pledges, wearing green and blue beanies, were gathered around a beer keg. Older, more confident, young men encircled them chanting, "Chug! Chug! Chug!" Revelers leaned against each other witnessing the activities, pointing fingers, and laughing as they raised their beer cups for a toast.

Those who were still partying at 3:30 in the morning didn't show any indication that they were ready to end the festivities. Johan stood on the second-floor balcony with other upperclassmen. He was feeling the effects of the Wapatui punch and the joint that was passed around the group. When thoughts of Annie popped into his head, he immediately dismissed them by participating in conversation.

Frank Mireles, the oldest member of the brotherhood, who should have graduated three years earlier, asked, "So, did you get any tonight?" He lit a Macanudo cigar and puffed on it until its end glowed bright red. Forming his lips into an open circle, he let out a smoke ring and offered the cigar to the group. Johan waved the cigar off; he wasn't much of a tobacco smoker.

Stepping out of the second-floor exit door, into the shadows of the oak tree, Luis inconspicuously joined the small gathering on the balcony. His emergence in the group, however, didn't stop Johan from responding.

"Maybe. It's just one of those nights. Sometimes you get some; sometimes you don't." He slid both hands in his jean pockets, body language cues for *I'm not offering any more info.*

Frank laughed, "Yeah, you did. You can't fake anything with me, bro!" He took another puff off the cigar and snickered.

***

Luis waved the puff of smoke away from his face, rested his elbows on the wrought iron railing, and listened to the conversation. A weak breeze faintly tousled his light brown hair. He wondered who Johan had been with. He knew that Annie and Johan had been dating, but his fraternity brother was notorious for inviting a girl to his room for an hour or two. Annie had left the party, so he considered the possibility that Johan could have been with someone else. Feeling uncertain about his role in the conversation, he chose not to participate and only listened.

***

Although Luis' face was silhouetted by a backyard spotlight, Johan acknowledged his fraternity brother's presence on the balcony with a nod and was careful with his response, "Well, I'm not saying yes, and I'm not saying no, and that's all I'm saying." He hoped he didn't give away too much. Knowing that Luis was dating Christy, and she was Annie's roommate, made him walk cautiously through the conversation. Normally he would brag about his bedroom encounters, but this one could get him into big trouble.

Somewhere in the crowd on the lawn, someone yelled out a fraternity "Hooyah!" This was a round up call for all pledges to gather in front of the caller, lineup, and prepare for orders. Steven McKenna, the pledge master, stood on the porch and waited for his men to assemble. Thirteen pledges lined up, removed their beanies, and held them to their hearts. "Pledges, hooyah!" Steven roared.

"Hooyah, Sir, hooyah!" They responded.

"Your night is over. Escort each other back to the dorms. No one drives; everyone walks. Hooyah!" Steven dismissed them with a wave.

"Hooyah, Sir, Hooyah!" With that, they positioned their beanies on the top of their heads and walked down the driveway in a single file by height, the tallest leading the way.

Johan watched the routine in the front yard and grinned as he remembered his own pledging season. He was the leader of his group and seemed to maintain that status among his pledge brothers. Others looked to him for example and guidance, and he knew it. His behavior tonight would be marveled at by some and condemned by many. He feared the condemnation of those who expected better from him. In the shadows of the balcony, he squinted his eyes and started scheming his plan for staying out of trouble with Annie.

:: 21 ::

Chapter 4

Lost Treasure

Annie braced herself against the shower wall as she slowly rose from the floor and took one last plunge into the jet stream. Her last attempt at cleansing. She reached for the silver knobs labeled hot and cold water and turned them at the same time, hoping to avoid a cold or hot blast. It worked. Taking her long dark hair into both hands, she wrung out the water then reached for her blue bath towel and proceeded to gently pat her face and shoulders. However, those parts of her body she thought might have deceived her tonight were raw from excessive soap and loofah. She quickly dried herself then slipped into her lounge wear.

Her thoughts and feelings struggled with each other and tangled up inside her head, making her feel confused. Longing for numbness, numbness of body and mind, everything was starting to feel too real. She knew she was going to have to tell her friends what she suspected. She couldn't keep this inside, but she didn't know how to articulate it. There was no soft way to say, "I think I was raped."

Would anyone believe me? Everyone likes Johan Menendez. He is the suave, intelligent fraternity man. He is worldly because he has traveled the world with his military family, and that makes him special in everyone's eyes. Her burdening thoughts weighed heavy in her mind. *No one will believe me. I'm a nobody. It was all my fault. I put myself in the situation.*

She hung her towel up on the bathroom hook and grabbed her party dress and panties off the floor. Walking into the bedroom, she was greeted by Maddie who gently enveloped her in a warm hug. Christy rose from her position on the bed, met them in the middle of the room, and encircled both girls. For a moment, no one spoke.

Annie felt a darkness move through her body. It started in her chest, spread to her head, and slid down into her stomach like the slow onset of a fever. She gently broke out of the group hug and quickly sat on her bed. Pulling her brown teddy bear blanket around her body, she closed herself off from her friends, focusing her eyes on the floor.

Christy and Maddie moved to their beds and sat quietly waiting for their friend to share what was bothering her.

Annie swallowed hard, making a loud gulping sound in her throat then spoke the words, "It wasn't my period." She hesitated. ". . . I think I was raped." The words fell like sharp pieces of shattered glass onto the floor. With the crashing sound echoing in her head, she felt her life was over. Her innocence was lost. She was ruined forever.

***

For a moment, Christy was at a loss for words. Her heart hurt for her beloved friend, but she didn't know what to do, how to help her. She always considered herself a smart girl, but no one ever taught her what to do in this kind of situation. She softly asked, "Annie, what happened?"

Maddie stared at the spot on the floor where Annie was looking, trying to keep from crying and searching to find the right words. Her mind felt frozen, her thoughts blank. She began to feel useless.

"It was Johan," Annie said in a dry voice, her eyes becoming small slits as she realized the gravity of the situation. Like a robot, spewing out words with no emotion, she recounted the events of the evening like reading off a list of facts. "I'm not exactly sure what happened. I wasn't drinking the trash-can punch. I had three cups of what Johan gave me, and the next thing I knew, it's two in the morning, I woke up in his bed, and my pantyhose were missing. I felt nauseous, and I just needed to come home." She looked from Christy then to Maddie, hoping they could somehow make the situation disappear.

"Why do you think something bad happened?" Christy held her breath.

Annie looked at Christy, eyes dark with pain. "Because I hurt, and I bled. He was standing over me when I woke up." After pausing for a moment, she added, "And why would I sleep at a party?" Her answers were firing out from her. She feared her sorority sisters wouldn't believe her. She needed them to believe her. "What should I do? Do I tell someone? What if they don't believe me?" She was starting to feel desperate then the realization hit her. "Oh, God! I took a shower!" Intense anger and debilitating fear crashed through her body as she realized she washed away the evidence.

Silence crept into the room and hung in the air like thick black smoke lingering after a raging fire as the three girls tried to process the truth. Annie had been raped by her boyfriend. She had no memory of it, and the evidence had been washed away. She curled deeper into the safety of her blanket.

Maddie walked over to Annie's bed, sat beside her, and wrapped her arms around blanketed shoulders. "Oh, no, Annie!" Maddie's voice ripped through the dark cloak of despair that shrouded the room. "I'm sorry." She hesitated to touch her friend, then held her gently anyway, hoping God would send her the right words to say.

Christy, still sitting on her own bed, laced her fingers together and thought. She considered whether to just bluntly ask what she was thinking or pick her words carefully. After a brief internal deliberation, she smoothed out any emotion in her face, a technique she learned in her court practice class, and asked, "Do you think he drugged you? Did you taste anything?"

Annie pulled the blanket tighter around her shoulders and said, "Well. I only had three glasses of punch, but he said they weren't spiked because there was another punch for those who didn't want alcohol. But the last one tasted a little salty. I thought maybe the salt was coming from me because we had been dancing up a storm." She didn't know who to look at as she made this revelation. She settled her eyes on Christy.

Meeting Annie's gaze for a moment, Christy swiveled in her chair and turned her attention to the red Macintosh computer resting on her brown metal desktop. She clicked on the blue AOL icon and drummed her fingers on the keyboard as she waited for the long dialup tone to indicate it was ready. With squinting eyes and body leaning in toward the screen, she blurted, "How do you spell Roofie?"

"I think it's R-O-O-F-I-E.   Or is it Y?" Maggie offered.

The annoying clickity click of the computer keys sounded as Christy's fingers flew. She wiggled the mouse, clicked on a few sites then leaned in to read the screen. Both Annie and Maddie waited silently as they watched the lines deepen in Christy's brow.

"Oh, Dear God. He roofied you. It says here that it only takes 30 minutes to kick in and can be tasteless or have a salty taste. It also says that a person can be out for hours depending on how much is given. What was the last thing you remember?" Christy's investigative nature and pre-law skills were kicking in.

Annie swallowed and cleared her parched throat. "We were dancing so much, I kept needing something to drink. The last drink was around 10:00. I remember checking the time on my watch." Her eyes scanned the ceiling as if she might find a memory there.

A piece of white dust fell from the popcorn ceiling, and Maddie watched it gently float like a feather to the floor. Holding back her tears she said, "Annie, that was the last time I saw you. You were dancing with him, and then I didn't worry because he was with you . . . I am so sorry. I didn't know you were in trouble. . . I'm sorry. . . I know we have a rule about not letting anyone go off with a boy, but I didn't think it was a problem because you two have boyfriends." This started the waterfall. The girls held each other and cried. The girlfriend's code was broken, and now one of them was hurt by a boyfriend, a perpetrator, a rapist.

Maddie broke from the circle first and meandered toward the bathroom searching for a tissue box. Christy joined in the search and found the blue Kleenex box behind a vanity mirror on Maddie's dresser. She pulled out a few sheets for herself then took the box across the room to her fallen roommate.

***

Annie laid back on her bed and curled up in a fetal position. She was spent. Her sobbing heaves had subsided, and there were no more tears to cry. She just needed to hug herself, rest for a moment, and think. Her thumb found its way to her mouth, and she vigorously began to chew her cuticle. With eyes fixed at a point between her two friends, she stared into space for a few minutes. Moving out of the dark spell that cast itself upon her, she blinked several times and spoke in a parched voice, "I was out for four hours. Do you two remember seeing him without me?" Annie, looking first at Maddie then at Christy, wanted to know what he had been doing all that time.

***

Christy noticed the distant look in Annie's eyes. She rubbed her cheeks with her hands and pursed her lips while she tried to remember. Shaking her head, Christy added to the night's scenario, "I saw him at the bar a few times without you. But I . . . Oh, God. I didn't think that . . . I didn't know." Taking Annie's ordeal quite personally because she was the eldest of the group and felt she should have watched out for her girls, she caught herself spiraling into a very sad place. She remembered watching after school specials when she was in high school about girlfriends who had separated at parties, resulting in one of them getting hurt. The creases around Christy's eyes deepened with sorrow and concern.

***

Maddie witnessed the sadness spreading across Christy's face and blurted, "Who knew he was such a disgusting person. He had all of us fooled. I don't know what we can do about it because it would be his word against yours." Maddie regretted saying that as soon it slipped past her lips.

***

"I know. . . I'm doomed. No one will believe me. No one," Annie said as she covered her feet. Closing her eyes to remove herself from the moment, in an exhale she stated, "I'm tired. . . I don't want to talk anymore. . . Can we just go to sleep? Maybe something will come to us in the morning." Annie leaned to her right and rested her head on her pillow.

***

Christy lifted her own pillow and found her pink pajamas. She also believed there was nothing they could do tonight. The light of tomorrow might bring new ideas. She nodded her head, shut the computer off, and smoothed out her bed covers.

***

Maddie turned down her bed, walked over to the light switch, and flicked it off, a routine signal for the roommates that the night was over. Not certain of what to feel or what to say, she saw Annie's sweet face in the moonlight and whispered, "We believe you, and we love you, Annie."

***

Annie smiled weakly, but the sadness in her big brown eyes was evident even in the thin slivers of light that passed through the Venetian blinds. She lay awake in her bed until her thoughts and clenching teeth wore her down.

Chapter 5

A Shame

Sunday morning was usually a happy time. The sorority sisters would dress in their Sunday best and attend a Catholic mass at the church near the university. Annie was reluctant to go. She lingered under the blankets while Maddie and Christy dressed.

"Do you want to join us? It might make you feel better," Christy asked as she tested the hair straightener, with her left index finger, to see if it was hot enough.

"Probably. I mean . . . it *might* make me feel better," Annie commented, her tone flat and depressed. She heard her own voice but couldn't hide her sadness. She was disappointed in herself for having gone to the party after her mother had warned her to stay away from fraternity houses. She was angry with herself for not being more aware of what was happening and for placing so much trust in someone, a fraternity boy. *How could I be so stupid*? She thought.

"Do you think he might be there? I am afraid to see him." Annie sat up in the bed, her hair a bird's nest, and looked to Christy for an answer.

"I doubt it. I'm sure he knows by now that you have an idea what happened. I bet he's going to be a big chicken and hide out." Christy examined her image in the mirror as she reached behind her head for an elusive strand of hair.

Maddie entered the room, humming to herself, with wet hair wrapped in a green towel and her blue terry-cloth bathrobe cinched at the waist. Sifting through her closet for a nice blouse to wear, she didn't notice that Annie wasn't dressed. She held up a lavender chiffon blouse to the light and turned to address her roommates. "What do you think about this one? Do you think it brings out my hazel eyes?" Spotting Annie sitting quietly on the edge of her bed, she lowered the blouse and softly asked, "Annie, I'm sorry. How are you feeling today?"

Annie knew her friends well. She expected Maddie to be her jovial self even early on a Sunday morning. Annie's smile slowly emerged because she couldn't ignore Maddie's good nature. "I'm okay, but I hurt." The sound and meaning of that word made her cringe inside.

"Oh, Annie. I'm so sorry," Maddie's tone changed. "If you don't want to go with us, I'm sure God will understand."

Annie scratched her nose then tucked herself deep into her plush blanket. "I think I'll stay home today. I need to think about things. . . Do you really think God will understand?" She whispered from deep within her comfort cave.

"Yeah. I do," Christy assured her as she retracted the cord on her hair blower and stuffed it and her hair products away in her bureau drawer.

Once Maddie tugged her blouse over her head and slipped her arms into the sleeves, she moved toward Annie, sat next to her on the bed, and sincerely asked, "Annie, would you like for one of us to stay with you? We can always go to a different mass?"

"No. I can't expect that from you, and I don't. Please go to mass. Please pray for me?" Annie asked, a lump developing in her throat.

Christy and Maddie each hugged Annie, and she smiled in return. She knew her friends were hurting with her, but she wanted them to know she was okay. The girls grabbed their purses and left the room, locking the door behind them.

Annie sat still, listening for the ding of the elevator down the hall to summon its arrival. She hesitated for a few minutes to make sure neither of the girls returned then she carefully rose from her bed. Keeping herself wrapped in her blanket, she shuffled over to the door and tested the lock. She wanted to be certain she was safe.

An emotional ache rose somewhere deep within her, adding to the soreness in her body. She felt as if she had over done a workout on a thigh machine at the university gym. Pressing her lips together to control her discomfort, she cautiously walked back toward her bed, stopped at her chest of drawers, and took the cosmetic mirror from its stand. With drawstrings loosened on her gray sweatpants, she pulled the elastic waist down to her knees and held the mirror to her thighs. Squeezing her eyes tightly closed until a wave of nausea passed, she looked down. Her reflection revealed a large red patch developing on her inner left thigh, but the bluish-purple stain on her other thigh made last night's events real. "Oh, gaw," she whispered to herself, ". . . It's true." An ugliness stirred up inside her that she had no strength to fight, so she couldn't prevent despair's dark shadow from attaching itself to her.

Moving slowly to her bed and gently settling on the edge, she felt alone with no one to turn to. She couldn't go to her mother, Angelita. This would mean admitting to doing something her mother warned against. Ana Maria De La Luz Cisneros had to campaign for the privilege of going to college then later again to live on campus. Because the family had one car, and they lived three miles from the closest campus, Angelita, with much hesitation, gave her oldest daughter her blessing.

The Cisneros family lived in a quiet neighborhood on a large lot filled with trees. Their two-bedroom home was consumed by five brothers, a sister, and her parents. A long closed-in patio lined with two sets of bunk beds and a trundle served as the boys' bedroom. She and her younger sister, Julia, shared a full-sized bed in a small room near the only bathroom. It was just too crowded to find any room or peace to study.

Annie knew that if she told her mother, she would make Annie return home, or worse yet, she would make her quit school. She understood her Hispanic culture. For the Cisneros family, it was more than eating beans and rice at every meal. There were rules about what girls could do and what exiting criteria must be met to leave the home. Girls were not supposed to go to college, and if they did, they were to become teachers or nurses. Girls could only leave the home if they were married. Girls were supposed to maintain their virginity until they married. She had broken all these rules, but the last one was the worst. Annie was disappointed in herself and the fact that she couldn't even hold on to her virginity. Being the first person in her family to go to college, she couldn't throw this opportunity away.

Clasping her hands in her lap, she rocked her body, an attempt to comfort herself as she did as a child. She struggled to think of ways to right the wrong that had been done to her. She definitely couldn't tell her brothers nor her father. The Cisneros men were proud men and prone to solve problems through physical means. She knew they would put their future on the line to set straight anyone who hurt her. Johan would be a dead man, and a Cisneros man would be in prison. She felt and believed this all the way down to her core. She needed to protect her family.

Shame rose its ugly head, and she tried to push it down, but there was a rottenness festering inside her, and it burned in her chest with a searing heat. She couldn't forgive herself for her part in last night's events and needed to decide how to deal with it. The conversation in her head bounced off the poster-clad walls of her dorm room as she articulated her thoughts through a dialogue with herself. She stared at a pink poster of a white kitten dangling from a tree branch with the slogan, "Just hang in there." Shaking her head, she looked past the kitten and spoke to the staleness in the air.

"Should I confront him?"

"What do I say?"

"Hey, you took something of mine, and I want it back!"

"Hey, you did something to me, and I don't like it!"

"Hey, you're an asshole, and I want nothing to do with you ever again!"

Like a rabbit caught in a trap, her eyes bulged, and her heart palpitated; she couldn't escape. The swishing sounds of her blood rushing through her ears and up her temples were deafening. She covered her face with her hands, struggling to stifle an emotional wave that was ready to overtake her. She knew this feeling; it had a name. She had encountered this brackish-brown monster several times in grade school.

A memory of her childhood returned to her as she sat alone in her dorm room. She saw herself at age seven returning home late from a friend's house. Her eldest brother, Samuel, stood in the living room with his legs apart and arms akimbo, holding a black leather belt in his left hand. He took it upon himself to whip her with their father's belt and grounded her from playing outside for a week.

The following day, little Annie, joining her younger siblings, Daniel, Adrian, Julia, and Mateo, for a backyard game of tag, had forgotten she was grounded. As quickly as the fun began, angry words cut through the laughter of children enjoying an afternoon before dinner time and bellowed out of the house. Annie whipped her head toward the porch and held her breath. The screen door slammed open. Samuel stood in the doorway with the black belt in his hand. He didn't even have to call her in. She knew what the cutting glare in his eyes meant, and she dared not meet it, or her punishment would be more severe.

He whipped her with more fury on the second day and yelled harsher comments for her disobedience. The words, "You-stupid-idiot! You-bad-girl!" were punctuated with a lash from the leather strap. Each would cut through her, leaving her feeling mangled and broken inside.

Over the sounds of whipping, her crying, and Samuel's rage-filled tirade, 12-year-old Tomas, her second oldest brother, shrank in the corner of the living room, shielding his eyes with his notebook from the sight of his precious little sister enduring their brother's wrath.

After Samuel finished, he sent her to her room where she hid in her closet and knelt on her knees. Her chest rose and fell with every sobbing heave then she calmed herself to a whimper as the red whelps on her bottom and the back of her thighs began to burn. Because she used her hand to block the belt from hitting her back, a red mark began to take shape on the tender skin of her inner arm. Annie felt so alone. So shattered with no one to help her gather up the pieces.

She stayed in her safe place until their mother returned home from work. No one spoke up for Annie; no one tattled on Samuel, who was fifteen at the time and viewed as an adult by all the smaller children. It was an unspoken code embraced by all those younger than Samuel. If anyone told their parents about anything he was doing, they would have to face him when their parents, Miguel and Angelita, were not around.

Annie's memory jumped to a second episode of shame that followed two years later. At the tender age of nine, it was her job to supervise her three-year-old brother, Mateo. It first seemed a simple task, for Mateo was her living doll. The game of pretend mother ended, however, when Mateo learned to walk and climb furniture, and Annie's autonomy changed. She had to take Mateo with her everywhere; she had no freedom to be a little girl.

One Saturday evening, while the family was watching *Welcome Back Kotter*, Annie took some time for herself to dance in front of her dresser mirror. She loved dancing; it filled her heart with joy like no other. Dance tunes from the radio filtered out the sounds of canned laughter emanating from the living room television. Annie gyrated, spun, snapped her fingers, mimicking the dance moves of Michael Jackson, and felt one with the music. Smiling at her image in the mirror and feeling good about herself, her special moment was quickly wiped away when her closed bedroom door abruptly slammed open, and her mother started yelling at her for not watching over her brother.

Angelita stood in the doorframe, her voice booming, "What do you think you're doing! You're supposed to be watching him!" She held Mateo by his right wrist, his mouth and hands covered in brown crumbs. "He ate a whole bowl of dog food because you weren't watching him! I can't believe it! It was your job! Take him and clean him up!"

Annie's heart rapidly sank down a deep well. She wanted to apologize, to explain, to ask for forgiveness. She didn't speak up for herself as that would have been viewed as defiance. Instead, she rapidly moved about taking care of her brother while the heavy talons of shame clawed her shoulders.

Sitting now in her dorm room, she took a deep breath. As she tried to muster up courage, shame stepped in and punched her in the gut. She couldn't change anything and didn't know if she was tough enough to stand up for herself. Instead, shame quickly pummeled her as negative thoughts started out against her. It happened so quickly. First it was a right jab, then a left hook and then a stunning blow. In an emotional boxing ring, helpless and down for the count, she was alone with no one in her corner, again.

Chapter 6

The Plan

Monday morning arrived too quickly, and Annie felt she had barely dozed off when her alarm sounded its strident call to attention. Sleepily reaching over her bed, she felt around for her clock on the desk and pressed the off button. The night was spent planning and practicing a dialogue in her head. It wore her down, and the exhaustion she had to fight clung to her.

Strength was needed, a kind she had never used before. This particular morning was important. She usually met with Johan at the dining hall for lunch after their 11:00 am classes. He was a geology major, and his building was on the west side of campus. Her American literature class was in the education building next to the outside patio of the lunchroom. She expected that he would show up for lunch like any other day, and she planned on having a conversation with him in public, and witnesses were needed just in case.

Lying flat on her back and staring up at the cracks in the ceiling, words and ideas began to align themselves into a plan. She rubbed her cheeks and mindlessly reached for a strand of hair that cascaded over her pillow. While in deep thought and chewing on her thumb, her mental planning was interrupted by Maddie's whistling.

"Whee, whee. Good morning, Annie. Are you going down to breakfast before class?" Maddie sat on her desk chair as she laced up her pink converse tennis shoes.

"No. Thanks, Maddie. I'm planning on meeting Johan after my last class," Annie said, trying to sound confident.

"Oh, wow! Do you want someone to be with you? I'll be done by 10:30," Maddie offered.

"We always meet at J2. I hope he'll show up." She moved from the comfort of her bed to her hard desk chair. "I'm pretty sure there will be plenty of people around." Sitting at her desk adjacent to Maddie's, she narrowed her eyes and avoided eye contact as she waited for a reaction from her roommate.

Maddie's lips tightened into a thin line as she took a deep breath in through her nose then softened into a weak smile when she breathed out. "I'm here for you, Annie. You don't have to do this alone. In fact, I'll skip class if you need me," Maddie offered.

"Thanks. I would like to have you around afterward. I just don't know what's going to happen or even what I'm going to say to him," Annie's voice quivered as she spoke. "I just have to go through this. I can't ignore it. I can't."

Maddie nodded her head, "Yeah. I agree. He can't get away with this." She stood and hugged Annie, and Annie welcomed the comfort. "I have to go meet Christy for breakfast before class. I'll see you later?" she asked.

"I'll come back here when we're done, but I don't really know what "done" means." Annie stood up and grabbed her backpack. "Are you leaving now? I'm going to head out."

"Yeah, I'll go down with you." Maddie grabbed her sunglasses from her bureau and slung her backpack over her shoulders.

They briskly walked down the hall and joined four other people waiting for the elevator. It screeched and moaned as it made its way down from the 14th floor. They all stepped in and rode the ten floors down in silence, everyone awkwardly avoiding eye contact and keeping a safe distance from each other. Although the elevator descended without stopping at any other floors, it jolted and shook as it slowed down on the street level. All the passengers looked at each other, and someone whispered, "Whew!"

"See you later, Maddie. Don't worry. I'm going to be okay," Annie assured her with a nod as if she was trying to convince herself, too.

"Okay." Maddie's weak smile re-appeared then quickly disappeared as Annie pushed her way out the glass doors and walked out onto the sidewalk. Maddie furrowed her brow in concern as she watched Annie walk away. Pushing a curl off her face and tucking it behind her ear, she turned and slowly walked toward the dining hall.

Seated at a small rectangular table in the cafeteria, Christy stirred nicely ripened banana slices into her oatmeal. She had a break between her 8:00 and 10:00 classes, so she took the opportunity to squeeze in a healthy breakfast. She watched Maddie saunter in and waved her spoon at her. Maddie spotted her roommate and wove her way through tables filled with students and backpacks.

"Hey, Christy. How was class this morning?" Maddie placed her backpack on an empty chair and sat in the seat next to her. She peered into Christy's bowl and added, "I see it's something healthy this morning."

"You know it," Christy smirked. "Class was good. Gotta love those philosophy courses. How was Annie this morning? Did she make it to class?"

"She did. She plans on talking to Johan after her 10:00 class."

"Really? By herself?"

"Yeah. They're meeting at J2. I asked if she wanted us with her, but she said no. She wanted to do this by herself. What do you think we should do?" Maddie leaned forward over the back of a chair, waiting for a response.

Christy hesitated before speaking, looked at her breakfast, stirred it for a moment, then said, "We stay close. Our girl is going to need us." Scooping her oatmeal up with her spoon then softly blowing on it to cool it, she started her breakfast routine of cereal and coffee. Christy could always be counted on to keep a level head and think through problems before reacting. She was a leader, and her sorority sisters admired this quality in her.

Maddie nodded and walked away to seek what would please her pallet. She had no breakfast routine other than to eat whatever she craved. Today it was pancakes and eggs. She grabbed a tray and stood in line at the country breakfast counter. A little brunette lady wearing a white chef's hat and burnt orange chef's smock stood with a small frying pan in one hand and a spatula in the other. Maddie stepped up, peered over the counter, and said, "I'll have two eggs over medium and a short stack of pancakes, please."

In the process of tying a plastic apron around his waist, a male student entered the serving area from a swinging door. Recognizing Maddie, a smile spread across his handsome face, and his big brown eyes brightened. "Hey, Maddie. How was psych class this morning?"

"Hey, Tristan. I have it at 9:30. You have Professor Feedler at 2:00, right?" she asked.

"Yeah. I got my project done late last night. Saturday's party went long." He grabbed a pair of metal tongs and a potholder from a shelf, lifted the lid of a warming tray, and placed three pancakes on a plate. "How late did you stay?" he asked. "I saw you a few times Saturday night, but I was so busy making sure the punch flowed and the music kept playing that I didn't get to hang out with anyone." He observed Maddie as she brushed red curls away from her face, revealing her hazel eyes. Making intentional direct eye contact with her, he placed her breakfast plate on the warm metal counter.

"Thanks. I stayed until 2:00. It was getting late, and we just needed to go home." She didn't want to say anything anymore. Tristan Doble was one of the fraternity brothers, and Maddie wanted to separate herself from that whole group of boys. She smiled at him, grabbed her plate and silverware, and walked away.

"Did you see Tristan?" Christy asked without waiting for Maddie to sit down.

"Yes, I did," Maddie replied. The cafeteria ambiance included dim lighting, smells of delicious foods, and background music. The Bee Gees' "How Deep is Your Love" started up with its instrumental and vocal harmonies, and it permeated through the room. Maddie caught herself in a brief reverie of herself gliding across a gym floor at a high school dance. She sat quietly at the table as she listened to the soothing voices of Barry, Robin, and Maurice.

Christy watched Maddie lose herself in the music. Maddie and Annie were such music lovers; they couldn't pass up a good song. Christy smiled at her friend who clearly was enjoying something in her mind. "Where did you go off to?" Christy finally interrupted.

"What? Oh," Maddie giggled. "I was in high school."

"I thought so," Christy laughed as she took a sip of her coffee. "Well, did you see Tristan?"

"I really don't want to talk to him right now. I think he likes me, but after this weekend, I don't think I want to have anything to do with those guys. What are you going to do about Luis? He's one of those guys," Maddie said cautiously. She knew her word choice was not going well.

"I know," Christy said in a flat tone. "I've been thinking about that." She breathed out heavily. "I'm not going to say anything to Luis just yet. I'll wait to see what Annie wants us to do. We might need Luis to remain on the sidelines. Depending on how Annie handles this, there could be some legal ramifications." Christy stared down at her coffee, wrapped her fingers around her cup to warm them, then looked up at Maddie.

Maddie sliced her golden pancakes into bite-sized triangles and poured a puddle of maple syrup over them. As she took a big bite, she turned her left wrist to look at her watch, and her eyes widened. With a mouth full of food, she said, "Wow! I'm running out of time." She swallowed her first bite as she prepared for her second and said, "I need to get to class so I can get a good seat." She continued to eat.

Christy added, "And it looks like you forgot your glasses again today, so you need to sit near the front."

"Yep. I did. I grabbed my sunglasses instead. I've gotta hurry. Are you going back to the room after your last class?" Maddie asked.

"Yeah. I will." She waited for Maddie to finish breakfast then both girls rose and walked over to the used utensil station. They dropped their silverware in the appropriate receptacle and stacked their dirty dishes on a tray. Stepping out of the dining hall and into the morning sun, they turned and gave each other a hug and took different sidewalks to their classes.

Chapter 7

All Arrogance

Johan Menendez was in his fourth year at the university with plans to graduate the following fall. The son of a military father and a school-teacher mother, he spent his high school years in Germany with his older sister Evonne. Although his family was Hispanic, he was fluent in both English and German and did not know the Spanish language. His understanding of Hispanic culture was limited to what he learned during his stay on campus. His tanned skin, dark eyes, and wavy brown hair led others to judge him as being a South Texas man, resulting in surprise when his friends spoke to him in Spanish, and he couldn't respond. It was a topic of conversation and the brunt of many jokes, but his ability to laugh at himself endeared him to others, so he had no problem making friends.

Joining a fraternity just seemed the practical thing to do, and his band of brothers believed and trusted in him. Others thought him smart and charming, which helped him build a reputation with the college girls, many who gave themselves to him willingly. Sometimes he had more than one girl on his hook at the same time. Annie, however, was the first local girl, and he liked her. She was different. She had conviction and an innocence he admired.

As he dressed for class, he inspected his image in the mirror. The whites of his big brown eyes were still bloodshot from all the weekend drinking and wading through smoke-filled rooms, so he grabbed a bottle of Visine and placed a drop in each one. Hoping to spread the drops over each orb, he blinked several times and shifted his eyes from left to right. A bottle of Copenhagen cologne, a Christmas gift from Annie, sat on a nightstand. He looked at it then decided he should wear it today. It might make her feel good that he cared enough to wear something she gave him. He sprayed it across his white polo shirt and pulled on a brown cardigan sweater, another gift from Annie.

In fact, Annie did many things for him. She bought him a landline phone and paid for his phone service. She purchased his groceries when she got paid from her work-study job, and sometimes she surprised him with little gifts here and there. He hadn't thought much about how he was going to handle today's conversation.

He didn't call her on Sunday because he had to sleep off Saturday's fun. Most of the house didn't settle down until 4:45 in the morning. By the time the police made their neighborhood rounds, the DJ had already packed up his vinyls, collected his weekend earnings, and headed home. The lawn gnomes with their booze-red noses and glazed eyes had started staggering up the street toward their dorm rooms at 4:30, missing the police by 15 minutes. All that remained for the police were house-dwelling fraternity brothers and a few girls who lingered in the living areas and kitchen of the house. Nothing to see here, folks.

Johan checked his breath by breathing into his cupped hand. "Eh," he said to himself, found it good enough, and shrugged his shoulders. He grabbed his textbook from the chipped coffee table in his room. The accompanying yellow spiral was wedged between the cushions of the faded brown tweed couch. When he pulled it out, it caught on a loose strand causing the first spiral to stretch and stick out, now becoming an ever-annoying spike. The curb-side couch was a talking piece for lady visitors, but it was seeing more wear-and-tear because of his spirals. Too late to worry about that now. He ran down the stairs and out the door toward his first class.

Chapter 8

Blurred Lines

Annie sat on the cold hard seat of a wooden desk, watching the time slowly tick its way toward 10:30. She loved American literature, and the lesson today was analyzing Nick Carroway of *The Great Gatsby*. She felt like Nick sometimes, the non-judgmental bystander. In the past three months she had attended various social events, and not knowing anyone, she participated in small talk, smiled, and did not partake in the libations. In the middle of her brief mental distraction, Professor Braidwood asked her a question, and she didn't hear it.

He was a tall, muscular man in his mid-thirties with well-trimmed dark hair and large, wide-set brown eyes that drew a person in. A chiseled jawline framed his features, making him a perfect stand-in for John F. Kennedy, Jr. He was the most attractive professor in the English department and had no problem filling his roster with wait-listed students.

Today he sat on his desk with one foot on the floor. In a deep, soothing voice he said, "Miss Cisneros, come back to us."

Startled, Annie said, "Huh? Oh, I'm sorry, Sir. Can you please ask me again?" She hoped she knew the answer.

"We were discussing Nick. What is some evidence in the reading that supports the assertion that he is the best character to serve as narrator for the novel?"

Whew, Annie thought, *I know this one*. "Fitzgerald makes sure to tell us through Nick, that Nick is a bystander. He does not have a deep relationship with anyone, yet everyone seems to open up to him. He can observe situations without bias. Evidence can be found throughout the novel to support this," she spoke with confidence. She was so glad she did her homework. "Would you like for me to go on?" She held her book in her hand and opened it to chapter three.

"First, let me say, you are correct. He is the best person as he connects with all the main characters and observes from the sides. But since we're out of time today, make sure you finish reading the novel and bring it with you on Wednesday along with a blue book. Be prepared for a timed writing. You will receive the prompt during class. Don't bother telling students in other classes as they will have a different prompt. See you Wednesday." Professor Braidwood rose from his position on his desk and began stuffing his satchel with books and papers.

As soon as class ended, Annie scooted out the back door trying to avoid anyone who wanted to speak with her. She stepped onto the sidewalk and headed toward the dining hall, trying to get there before Johan. She wanted to be seated and in control of herself because the thought of seeing him revolted her, causing her stomach to lurch.

She entered Jesten Hall and slowly took the stairs up to the second floor. The heavy brown doors to the dining hall were wide open, so she walked through the threshold and visually scanned the room for a good table. Spotting a small round table for two next to a large window situated adjacent to the entrance, she made her way over to claim it. Her plan was to know exactly when he was walking up and not be taken by surprise.

Annie placed her backpack on the floor and rested it against the tinted window. Glancing out past the large oak tree in the courtyard, she watched Johan confidently walking toward the building. Her heart palpitated in her chest, and she felt heat rush up to her ears. Taking a deep breath, she placed both hands on the table to ground herself, but sweat from her palms made its impression on the laminate, giving away her secret. With the left sleeve of her pink sweater, she wiped the table then rested her hands in her lap. Anxiety crept in through her thoughts, causing her legs to shake and her breathing to turn erratic. She took two more deep breaths and tried to breathe rhythmically. Then he walked in.

For a moment she held her breath and pursed her lips as she watched him glance about the hall, his tall frame darkening the doorway. Racing in her chest, her heartbeat defied her as it lost its rhythm and caused her to now doubt that she could confront him. She whispered to herself, "Lord, help me."

Johan flashed a smile of straight top teeth and crooked bottom teeth and meandered over to the pedestal table. Annie didn't return the smile. He leaned over to kiss her on her left check; she received it but did not reciprocate. He stepped back looking at her, nodded his head, and sat in the chair across from her. She kept her hands folded in her lap. Like an old train slowly clickety, clacking through a railroad crossing, silence seeped between them.

"How are you? Sorry I didn't call yesterday. I was really busy," Johan said, trying to sound convincing.

Annie hesitated before she spoke. She struggled with placing her gears in autopilot or picking her words carefully. In a fraction of a second, she decided to pick her words carefully and not let her emotions override her.

"We need to talk about what happened on Saturday," she spoke clearly and firmly.

"What? What do you think happened?" he asked, settling back in his chair and spreading his legs.

"You hurt me," she said.

"What? No. I didn't do anything with you that you didn't want to do," he stated.

"What? What do you think I wanted?" she demanded.

"You asked me to take you to my room and do stuff," he said while keeping his composure. His voice was steady with no emotion. There were too many people around.

"What? And I just fell asleep on your bed after doing something I had never done before in my life? No. I don't think so," she kept her voice low.

"You were all over me. You can ask anybody. I just tried to save your reputation and took you to my room. YOU came on to me, so I gave it back to you." He leaned back in his chair.

"No . . . None of this makes sense," her voice rose, and a couple sitting behind them looked in their direction. Johan waved them off.

"Johan, it was not like that. Something was wrong with me. I remember feeling dizzy, and that's all I remember." Annie shook her head in disbelief.

"You were drunk."

"I was what? I wasn't drinking anything but punch, and YOU gave it to me. YOU did."

"Maybe you got some on your own."

"No, Johan. YOU brought me the punch every time. I didn't get my own drinks. I trusted you."

"I gave you your drinks, yeah, but I didn't put anything in them."

"Who said you put anything in them? I didn't say that. Johan! What did you do to me?

"I did nothing to you. Nothing. You acted weird, I took you to my room, and you started taking my belt off. Then one thing led to another. YOU wanted it."

"No," she whispered loudly. "No. I didn't. Why would I give myself up like that?" It was more a statement than a question.

"Yes. You did," he said matter-of-factly.

Annie knew he was wrong and felt revolted by the whole conversation. She was ready to get up and leave the table when he spoke again.

"If you try to tell anyone this story you're making up, I'll go tell your parents what you have been up to."

"What? My parents?" she asked.

"Yeah. I'm sure your parents would like to know that you were at a fraternity party, got drunk, and slept with a fraternity boy. It won't even matter who you slept with; they'll be pissed either way."

She couldn't believe it. He turned everything on her. She wanted to cry. She wanted to scream and beat him. She even wanted to jump out the window. Instead, she sat still, kept her composure, and looked away from him. "I think it's time for you to go. Please leave."

"Hell, no. I'm hungry. I'm going to get something to eat. Do you want anything?" He rose from the table and waited for a response.

She turned her head away from him as he headed to the buffet station. At his departure, she caught his reflection in the window and watched him and his arrogance strut away while she cringed and pushed down the urge to sling her backpack against the back of his head. She saw him casually pick up a dinner plate and pick out his silverware.

Annie scooped up her backpack and hurried out of the cafeteria. He had confused her; she wasn't prepared for that. She was beginning to doubt herself and what she knew. She rushed up the emergency stairs to the next floor and took the elevator the rest of the way. She didn't want him coming after her. She just ran. She ran in her heart. She ran in her head. She ran and ran.

***

With his tray in hand, Johan returned to the table and found it occupied by another couple. He wasn't surprised that Annie left; he expected it. Finding another empty table, he sat down to eat his fried chicken, French fries, and okra, with a chaser of Big Red. Greetings of nods and waves passed between him and fraternity brothers enjoying the campus' fine dining.

After his meal, he decided to return to the fraternity house. Johan felt confident that he had Annie where he wanted her. She was his now. He believed that he would be able to manipulate her, and no one would ever know the truth. A smile spread over his face as he neared the yard and saw the white curtain of his bedroom window billow out then back in again. He was going to get his reading done for the night and call her later.

Chapter 9

Run Away

Annie ran up to the third floor and caught the elevator there. Its sluggish chug, chug ascended, coming to a complete stop in front of her. It dinged and, with hesitance, opened its doors to welcome her. Relieved that it was empty, and Johan hadn't ridden it up from the lobby, she sighed and quickly stepped in and extended one shaking finger to press the "close door" button, in an attempt to hurry the process. However, the steel panels took their sweet time, and she panicked like a small bird caught in a storefront window. With her eyes wide and a growing hypervigilance, she couldn't let her guard down until she was alone. The screeches and groans of the elevator pulleys and chains synced with the sounds trapped in her throat. She stared at the door anticipating an intruder at any time as the cart traveled upward toward her safe place.

Once in her hall, she hurried out of the elevator to avoid having to chat with any of the five girls waiting to switch places with her. She hurried down the carpeted corridor toward her room as she automatically searched for her keys in the outside pocket of her burnt-orange plaid backpack, a gift from her sister. The clinking of her keys announced her presence at the door as her trembling hand tried to connect the key with the lock.

The room was dark and cold, a perfect cave for escape. She flung her backpack toward her bed, and it landed on the floor next to her desk. Kicking off her Keds, she crawled onto her bed and rested her head on her pillow, hoping to stay like that forever. For a moment, she had nothing on her mind. The vacuous mental space gave her a chance to breathe and rest. Needing a reprieve from the stress and out of emotional exhaustion, she fell asleep.

Chapter 10

Forged Confidence

After hiding behind clouds most of the day, the sun peeked through the blinds next to Annie's bed, lapping her face with warmth. She stirred and felt like she had slept all day. The springs in her mattress creaked as she rolled over and squinted toward her desk to focus on the white numbers of her alarm clock. She witnessed the little automated tiles flip from 3:59 to 4:00. Catching the tiles in the act of moving the day forward always seemed like magic, like time stood still for a moment just for her. She expected Christy and Maddie to burst through the door at any moment, deep in conversation.

Just as she expected, she heard their excited voices as they walked down the hall. Then the voices softened and hushed as a key turned in the deadbolt and the door slowly opened. The lights were out in the room, and the afternoon sunlight streamed in lines through the blinds.

Christy whispered, "Annie, are you here?"

"Yes, I'm on my bed. You can come in. Turn on the lights." Annie sat up, her hair disheveled and mascara smudged under her eyes.

Maddie flipped the switch and the ceiling fan, and its three light bulbs buzzed into action. "Hey," she softly said. "How are you?"

"I don't know. . . I don't know anything. . . Can we talk before we go to dinner?"

"Of course," Christy asserted as she sidled over to her bed and sat on the edge, slowly kicking off her shoes.

"Sure," Maddie said comfortingly while she pulled her chair away from her desk and gingerly sat on the hard wooden seat.

Hardly knowing where to start, Annie took a deep breath and began. "Well, he showed up for brunch. I got there before he did because I wanted to have some kind of control over the situation. He tried to kiss me, but I couldn't kiss him back. I didn't wait to talk about Saturday. I just went right for it. But he pretty much insisted that it was my fault. He denied that he did anything wrong. He even denied putting anything in my drink, but I hadn't even brought that up. Then he threatened to tell my parents. . . He threatened to tell my parents," she repeated. "He said he was going to tell them I did things at the party." Annie looked at her sisters and added, "I can't let him tell my parents. That will ruin me. My parents will make me come home; I'll have to quit school." She paused to catch her breath. "He's such a good liar; he'll convince them of things. I know it. I know it." She stared past her roommates imagining the horror that would come because of the whole situation.

"Annie, he's evil. What if you went and told your parents the truth?" Maddie suggested.

"No! I can't! This is shameful! My parents would flip, and my dad and brothers would set out to hurt him. I know this. Plus, it's his word against mine. I'm a nobody on this campus; no one would believe me. . . I don't want to disappoint my family," Annie's voice trembled at the realization of what she was saying.

Christy stood and moved to her desk, elongating her back and making herself appear authoritative. "Annie, what can we do for you? How can we help you?"

"I don't know. I feel really lost, like I have no power or control over any of this," Annie said defeatedly and stared at the floor.

Maddie cast her eyes to the floor as she mentally searched for the right words to say. A thickening silence filled the gap between all three girls as no one could offer a defense plan. She crossed her long legs and mindlessly wiggled her toes.

Annie spotted her alarm clock, and for the first time, observed the time tiles change twice in one day. She knew she couldn't expect her friends to have the answers. This was a new situation for them, too. She was the first to speak up after what seemed like an eternity, "You know. I hope he knows our relationship is over. He acted like nothing had happened. But I didn't make sure to end it because his attitude threw me off."

Christy tilted her head to the side and squinted as she carefully spoke, "Annie, that's important. He needs to know the relationship is over. It is over, right?"

Annie quickly turned to her and adamantly said, "Of course."

"Okay, then," Maddie added. "That's the next step, to make sure it ends. With it over, he'll have no more control over you."

"Right," Annie agreed, although she didn't quite feel confident that she had the strength to put an end to this horrible time in her life.

There was a significant lull in the conversation as the girls sat quietly in the moment, letting the realization of the seriousness of the whole situation solidify. After three minutes of silence, the topic of Johan seemed to be over, so Christy suggested, "How about we go eat dinner now? I have a lot of homework, and I want to get back to it." She pointed a finger first at Maddie then at Annie and added, "Don't either of you let me get distracted from doing my essay tonight."

Annie said, "I'm not hungry. You two go without me."

Maddie adamantly piped in, "Oh, no you don't. You're not going to start skipping out. I bet you haven't eaten all day." It was evident she was not going to let Annie wallow in sadness and neglect herself. She stood and held out a hand to Annie.

Annie took Maddie's hand and allowed herself to be pulled to her feet. She thought about her friend's comment and realized she did not eat anything on Sunday either.

"I haven't," Annie conceded. "You're right. . . Let's go." She crossed over to her desk and slipped on her shoes. Taking her hairbrush from her desk drawer, she passed it through her long dark strands, and said, "I'm ready."

Maddie said, "Wait." She grabbed a tissue and a small jar of cold cream from her desk. Turning to Annie, she ordered, "Come here. We can't have you going to the dining hall looking like a raccoon." She laughed as she opened the jar, scooped out a small dollop with the tissue, and wiped the dark smudges from under Annie's eyes.

Annie smiled then led the girls out of the room, trying to take control over something.

Chapter 11

Some Confusion

No one knew exactly what was growing in Annie's mind. Although the week passed without incident, Annie's thoughts about herself had shifted. The shame and guilt that mastered her life convinced her that she was now a tainted girl and that no decent man would ever want her because she was no longer a decent young lady. Her dreams of marrying a good man were now marred, and she feared that anyone she dated would be disappointed in her since she was no longer a virgin. She was a tarnished young woman now. She was flawed beyond repair, and no one would want her. No one.

On Friday after her last class, she returned to her dorm room, fumbling with her keys, she could hear the phone ringing inside. She hurried to unlock the door then dashed to her desk. Thinking it might be her mother, she picked up on the fifth ring and said, "Hello?"

There was a slight hesitation on the other end, then a male voice spoke out, "Annie?"

She recognized it right away and said, "Johan, why are you calling?"

"I thought maybe we could talk. I missed you this week," his voice was sad and sincere.

"I don't know what to say," she commented. She was a bit confused and wondered why he was talking like that.

"Annie, I need to see you. You mean a lot to me. I don't want to end our relationship," he added. "Can we meet tonight?"

"What? Tonight? Why?" she asked.

"Let's just talk. Okay? Let's just see each other and take it from there." His soft tone sounded like he wasn't ready to end the relationship.

There was a dull silence on her end of the line as she thought about his request. The kindness in his voice was like the Johan she fell in love with. This confused her. Her heart started to pick up its pace in its march in her chest, so she tried to slow her breathing down.

"Annie? Don't hang up. Please," he pleaded.

"Why shouldn't I?" It was a rhetorical question.

"Because I need to talk to you." He hesitated. "I'm sorry about everything. I want to make it up to you." Another hesitation. "I love you," he said and waited for her response.

Annie paused then asked, "What? You want to be with me?"

"Yes. Can we talk tonight? I can meet you on campus. We're just gonna talk," he assured.

Annie sat on the edge of her chair, swallowed hard, and thought about a well-lit area in the open where they could meet. She didn't want to stray too far from the dorm. A seed of dismay grew in her head, the one that told her that she was ruined, and no other man would want her. She was stuck. "Why don't you just come to Jesten. We can meet in the lobby at 10:00."

"Okay. I love you, Annie," he said it again then returned the receiver to its cradle.

***

The smug self-confidence that walked with him everywhere he went increased his certainty that he was going to be able to convince her to stay with him. He believed he loved her, but that was not the concern. He needed HER to believe it.

He looked around his room and decided to tidy up in case their evening ended up at the fraternity house. Taking the glass ashtray from the coffee table, he dumped the ashes of a used joint in a small wicker waste basket and used the palm of his hand to scrape crumbs and dust from the tabletop into the can. He then unlatched the lock to the single-hung window next to the telephone table and pushed the lower pane up to air out his room. He did the same to the window next to his bed. He didn't want her to know how much he had been partying.

Branches of the large dark oak tree outside his second-floor bedroom swayed as a cool breeze blew through one unscreened pane and exited out the second window. Johan followed it and climbed out the portal by his nightstand to sit on the roof of the first floor. It was peaceful out there. From the rooftop he could see up the meandering street to the university. Students were strolling to and from campus, and sounds of laughter could be heard from several houses away. He spotted Luis sauntering down the main road toward the house, and a bit of concern creeped into his thoughts as he wondered what Luis knew. Johan's foot slipped on a brown roof tile, and his presence on the gable spooked a gray pigeon. The unwanted winged visitor frantically took flight, and the susurrus of its departure startled other birds in the trees. The wing flapping calmed as the frightened pigeon joined its band hidden among the multi shades of green and brown of the mighty oak. Johan returned to his bedroom before he called too much attention to himself.

Chapter 12

Comfort Food

Annie's stomach growled for the third time in an hour. She had skipped lunch and now had to wait for the dining hall to open for dinner. Spying an open bag of chips sitting on Maddie's desk, she walked over to it, picked it up, was tempted then changed her mind. *Not nice to eat someone else's food,* she thought. Instead, she filled her drinking cup with tap water and drank it down in one breath. She expected her roommates to burst through the threshold of their dorm room at any moment.

Like clockwork, she heard their chatter as they made their way down the hallway. The door opened, and the two slender girls entered at the same time. "Hi, you two," Annie spoke first.

In a chorus, they both responded, "Hey, Annie!" causing them to break out into sudden laughter.

"Hey! Pinch. Poke. You owe me a coke," Maddie chimed as she made her way to her bed.

Christy exclaimed, "I promise to get you one in the dining hall." Turning her attention to Annie, she asked, "How are you doing?"

"I'm good. I've just been relaxing," she quickly replied, trying to sound convincing. She so wanted to tell them about her conversation with Johan, but a voice in her head whispered, *"You better not. Don't do it."* She smiled at them as she adhered to it and decided not to say a word.

"Is anyone hungry?" Christy asked.

"Me!" Maddie shouted.

"I'm a little hungry," Annie sheepishly responded. She didn't know why she didn't just say she was starving. She avoided eye contact with her roommates as keeping the secret about seeing Johan later was making her uncomfortable.

Annie slipped on her Dr. Scholl's wooden sandals, a graduation gift from her Tia Blanca, slid her meal card into the back right pocket of her blue walking shorts, and was ready to head down to the dining hall. Christy and Maddie flung their backpacks onto their beds, and in unison they all said, "Let's go."

The dining hall on the second floor was slowly filling with hungry students, and the buffet lines were forming. Annie volunteered to find a table while the other two chose their buffet lines. She held her breath and with wide eyes scoured the room for any Delta Phi fraternity brothers. When she felt the coast was clear, she sighed and let the tense muscles in her face relax. However, she didn't want to relax completely because she felt she needed to stay on guard in case she had to flee the room.

Maddie returned to the table with a plate of golden fried chicken, creamy macaroni and cheese, and a side of green beans. "Go ahead, Annie. I've got the table now."

"Okay. Where's your drink?" Annie asked.

"Christy owes me. Let's see if she remembers," Maddie laughed.

Annie giggled, "Okay. Let's see. I'll be back." She left the table to find the Chinese buffet.

***

Christy stood in a slow-moving buffet line. She was hoping to get a good piece of grilled fish and a nice-sized baked sweet potato. She was never one for processed or junk food, so she tried to eat healthily whenever possible. She tippy-toed to peer over the muscular, dishwater- blond boy in front of her. The buffet line also offered a side salad and a rainbow of steamed vegetables in orange, red, and various shades of green. *Perfect*, she thought. "I've got to remember Maddie's coke," she said aloud to herself.

"What?" the boy in front of her turned to her and asked. He flashed a pearly white smile. His eyes were greenish/blue and sparkled with kindness.

Christy was surprised at his handsomeness. "Oh, no. Sorry. I was talking to myself." She tried to mask her intrigue by keeping her eye contact brief.

"Oh, okay. Hey, I'm Derek Doss. You are?" he asked.

"Oh, hi. I'm Christy," she offered.

"Nice to meet you. You come here often?" he laughed.

Christy noticed the melodic sound in his laughter. It was genuine and kind. *Is he flirting with me?* She thought as a slight squint in her left eye quickly flashed.

She laughed with him, and a smile spread across her face. *He seems like a nice guy.*

Derek turned his attention back to the serving counter as he was next in line. Christy watched him order the exact same meal she was planning. *Hm. And he eats healthily, too.* Her curiosity was growing like a dandelion in a field, wild and free. She mentally blew on it and sent it to the wind. Placing her meal order with the meal attendant, she moved to the end of the serving counter to retrieve her dish. With her tray in hand, she turned and found she had to sidle between queues of hungry students to get to the fountain drinks. Dispensing iced water for herself and coke for Maddie, through her periphery, Christy watched Derek take a windowed seat at an available table for two. *Maybe he's with no one,* she thought. She shook her head to dismiss her interest and ambled back to the table.

"Here you go. I owe you nothing now," she said as she handed Maddie an ice-cold beverage in a blue plastic tumbler. Taking her seat, she quickly scanned through the room and spotted Derek sitting in her line of vision. *There he is again.* "Hey, don't look now, but do you know the guy sitting alone by the windows?" she asked.

Like a three-year-old child doing exactly the opposite of what she's been told, Maddie turned her head and craned her neck to catch sight of the young man who was mystifying her friend. "Nope. I have no idea. What about him?" she asked as she spooned macaroni into her mouth and chased it down with a swig of her drink.

"Oh, it's nothing. I just met him in line. He seemed really nice." She took her napkin and placed it across her lap. "I see you started eating before grace. . . I guess it's okay. If we wait for Annie, our food will get cold; she can be in a long line. Let's just eat, and we'll say grace when she gets back."

Maddie shrugged her shoulders, nodded, and continued eating, following each bite with a sip of soda.

At the fifth serving station, Annie found the perfect comfort food: fried rice, sesame chicken, and crab Rangoon. Today was her lucky day. Her salivary glands watered, and she could feel their slight tug on the sides of her throat. *Oh, please don't let them be out of anything. Oh, wait, dinner just started; everything should be available.* She really needed something good to eat, and Chinese food was her best friend when she was feeling defeated. She quickly grabbed a red plastic tray from a stack near the counter. Stepping up to put in her order, she spotted Tristan behind the serving station. Her smile froze, and for a split second, she was speechless.

"What would you like?" Tristan's question was somewhat robotic and practiced.

"I'll have the number two dinner with a side of Rangoon," her voice cracked. She watched him serve her dish and hoped he wouldn't ask her any questions. He didn't, and he slid her plastic receptacle down the tray slide to the end of the counter. Her plate was ready, and with little beads of sweat forming on her upper lip, she scooped up her dish and escaped to her table with her friends, a safe zone.

Christy and Maddie were leaning in toward each other deep in discussion when Annie joined them. She scooted into a chair across from the empty seat at the four-person table. Swiftly wiping the sweat from her lip before either of them noticed, she asked, "What are you two whispering about?"

Maddie piped in, "Oh, Christy was asking about that boy sitting alone by the windows. Do you know him?"

Annie nonchalantly responded, "Oh, yeah. I think his name is Darin or Daryl. I don't remember. I met him freshman year during orientation. But that's all I know. What about him?"

"I don't know. I just met him. His name is Derek Doss," she shared.

"Oh, yeah! Derek," Annie exclaimed.

"Well. I just thought he was nice," Christy said, ending the conversation by pressing her hands together for prayer and crossing herself. Both girls followed, and they sat in reverence as each prayed silently, in the warmth of the fading sun.

***

On the other side of the windows, the sun shifted out from behind a cloud, and Derek sat as a silhouette against the light. The girls didn't notice the smile that brightened his countenance as he watched them pray. Taking a chance that one of them would notice his attention, he observed them anyway. He recognized one of the girls as a girl he met at orientation, but he had not encountered her in any of his classes. She was hard for him to forget because of her adorable, sweet face, sunny disposition, and long dark hair. Now he saw another side of her, a prayerful side, and admired her even more.

Chapter 13

Atypical Friday

Friday nights held the promise of relief from a stressful week and an opportunity to socialize with other friends. Tonight, a fellow sorority was having a dance, and Maddie and Christy were sure to attend.

"Annie, do you want to go with us tonight? You know how you love to dance. I'm sure it'll be lots of fun," Maddie said encouragingly. She was dabbing her Halston perfume behind her ears and on the pulse points on her wrists. She wore her best fitting Calvin Klein jeans, a white polo, and white Kaeppa tennis shoes, the ones with the double laces. Her hair was up in a ponytail, and her lips were highlighted by pink lip gloss.

Her appearance made Annie smile. "You look so cute!" Annie commented. "You look like you're ready for a full night of dancing, and I hope they play the best songs for you."

Giggling like a schoolgirl, Maddie said, "Thanks. I guess this means you're not going."

"I'm not. I think I'll sit this dance out, but have fun for me," she exclaimed.

Christy stepped out of the bathroom dressed for the evening in gray walking shorts and a striped pink and gray blouse. She piped into the conversation, "Aw, Annie. It won't be the same without you. I love to watch you dance."

"Girls, you are too good to me. Please just have fun. You can tell me all about it when you get back," Annie responded. "Remember the buddy system," she added.

Maddie and Christy found their school IDs and room keys, waved to Annie, and stepped out for the night.

Annie sat upright at her desk and fiddled with her school ID. She flipped it from edge to edge then looked at her picture. Her image reflected a happy girl, grinning from ear to ear. It was an innocent girl with dreams and aspirations, smiling back at her. Annie had moved so far away from that person. In just the course of a week, her life, confidence, and self-image had changed. There was a darkness inside her now, one that she could see when she cast her eyes on her own image in the mirror on her desk.

The evening moved slowly into night as sunlight in the room shifted to moonlight. The slats on the blinds cast their shadows against the wall over Maddie's bed. Annie watched them and imagined herself in a jail cell. She was locked up, away from society, but not away from herself. She rose from her chair and walked over to her bed. She sat then leaned back with her legs dangling from the mattress. She turned her gaze to the ceiling, hands tucked behind her head. She thought she could lie like that forever. Her mind wandered from image to image as she tried to remember events from the weekend before. She had scoured every part of the video in her mind. Nothing new ever developed.

Her alarm clock turned its tiles to 9:30; it was a long time before her roommates would return from the dance. Annie thought maybe she would read a few more chapters in her novel before they returned. She reached back to grab her book from the small white shelf above her bed. Like the perfect timing of a synchronized dance, her phone rang. She quickly rose and rushed to her desk. Without thinking, she answered the call. "Hello?"

"Hello, Mi hijita. It's Mom. Are you busy?" Hearing her mom's voice both startled and comforted her. She could hear a brightness in her tone, and the thought of her mother's smile put a genuine smile on her own face.

"Hi, Mamita. I am not busy. It's so good to hear from you." Annie was sincere.

"I know it's Friday night, and you're probably getting ready for a dance."

"There is a dance tonight. We're not putting it on; it's the Alpha Tau Zetas."

"Oh, you are the BELs, right? The Beta Epsilon Lambdas?"

"Yeah. You got it."

"Well, I just wanted to see how your Spring semester was going. I haven't heard from you in a few weeks."

"Everything is good, Mommy. I like my classes." This was the truth.

"Good. Something inside me just told me I needed to call you. I'm always thinking of you, mija, and you know you can always talk to me if things get tough."

"Thank you, Mommy," Annie said this but knew in the back of her mind that there were some things she just couldn't share.

"Okay. Well, I'm just checking on you," Angelita assured, with a voice full of love for her daughter.

"I'm okay. Are you okay?" Annie turned the attention away from herself. Deflection.

"Yes. We are all good here. School has everyone busy, and I'm cooking up a storm. There are always mouths to feed," Angelita laughed.

Annie loved her mother's laugh. It was genuine, unique, and heartwarming. There was always music in her mother's voice, a soothing, light-hearted melody that drew a person in and made them feel welcomed. Her tune, though, like a symphony, could crescendo to reflect her disappointment or anger. Tonight, there was none of that. The melody was smooth and upbeat. Normally, this would reset Annie's own mood, but the anxiety over the upcoming appointment loomed like the dread over an anticipated vaccination. It was never a little pinch.

"Okay, mi amor. We'll talk real soon," Angelita promised.

"Yes. We will. Good night, Mommy," Annie chimed.

"Good night. Have fun. Y que Dios te bendiga." Angelita hung up the phone first.

Although Annie knew her mother loved her, the words "I love you" were never passed between the two of them. She never understood this and longed to hear her mother say the words. Perhaps she did when she was a child, but the phrase went unused during her teen and young adult years. Annie vowed to herself that she would use those words with her own children.

The phone rang again barely two minutes after she hung up with her mother. "Hello?" Annie's body began to shake, and her breathy voice almost exposed her fear to the caller.

"Annie, it's me. I'm in the lobby. I'll wait here." Johan had arrived on time and was calling from the front desk of the West Wing.

"Okay. I'll come down." Annie hung up the phone, found her room key, and slipped into her shoes. She moved swiftly as she tried to put herself emotionally in a place where she felt nothing.

When the elevator doors hesitantly opened to the first floor, Johan was standing on the other side with a single red rose clad in thorns, bug-eaten leaves, and withered petals. Annie imagined he picked it from someone's yard on his way up the street.

"Hi. I'm glad you came down," he said through a Cheshire-Cat grin.

"Okay. I'm here. Let's go over to the table by the windows to talk." She led the way to the square table adjacent to the front desk. They took seats across from each other.

Johan placed the rose in front of her. She didn't touch it. Although in the past she would have found the gesture sweet and romantic; at the moment, it revolted her.

"What do you want to talk about?" She asked.

"I want to talk about us. I am really sorry about everything. I'm sorry things happened. I'm sorry I didn't comfort you when you were feeling bad," he spoke cautiously.

Were feeling bad? She thought. She could see that he was being careful with his words, and she noticed his tone was low, seeming sincere.

He paused as the words sank in. "Annie, I love you. I have come to realize that after the last few days, and I know that you love me."

He was right; she did love him, but it wasn't the same.

Annie tried to read his face. She witnessed his brown eyes tear up as he gazed directly into hers. She was drawn to the old Johan, the one she knew. Her mind switched back to Annie from two weeks before, and she felt that he really meant what he was saying.

"Can you forgive me?" he asked.

Annie took a moment to think about it then said, "Johan, I trusted you. I expected you to take care of me, not take advantage of me." The words rolled across the table like craps dice, tumbling and spinning in different directions with an unpredictable outcome. She couldn't hide the emotion in her eyes.

"I'm sorry. I'm so sorry," he whispered.

Annie believed him. He gently squeezed her hands in his, a comforting, sincere gesture. She closed her eyes and held back hot tears that were swelling and preparing to spill over. She felt she had been sitting in her chair for hours, but only a few minutes had passed. After her bubbling emotions settled in her chest, she asked, "What do we do now?"

"We can start over. I promise never to hurt you again." His eyes grew large and sad like a puppy's eyes after it's been caught destroying flowers in the garden.

She nodded her head but couldn't speak. Everything was happening so fast. Colors of black, blue, green, and red sifted through her head. Attached to them were thoughts of *there is no one else for me*. This was her destiny. She would just have to accept that she was a changed woman, Johan was the man who changed her, and she had to stay with him.

***

As the evening light traded places with the night shift, students began to filter in and out of the lobby. The cadence of excited voices neared and fell away from the study room. Johan was finding it difficult to keep focused on his conversation with Annie as fellow fraternity brothers would stop by to greet them. If he was going to continue his visit with Annie, he needed to make a suggestion for a quieter place to talk, his bedroom. He had a window of opportunity to guide her in the direction that he needed her to go, and he didn't want to miss it.

"Hey, I really want to continue this conversation, but it's starting to get very busy here. What do you say we go back to the fraternity house. It seems that most of the guys are in this dorm anyway," he coaxed.

***

Annie also wanted to continue talking. Before the incident occurred, she and Johan were good friends with very strong feelings for each other. "Okay. Maybe just for an hour. I don't want to stay out late tonight, and we can just sit in the living room," she insisted and rose from her seat. He quickly joined her and led her out the glass doors.

They walked across campus with oak leaves crunching under their feet. Occasionally, a squirrel, running home to its drey, tardy for dinner, scurried past them. *Maybe tonight would be the night we spot the illusive white squirrel,* Annie thought.

The elements of the night felt so familiar. A soft breeze rustled the leaves in the trees, and an owl hooted in the distance. A light whiff of ginger and cardamom tickled her nose and reminded her of her mother's array of trees in the family's front yard. She couldn't remember the name of the big white blossoms that bloomed every spring. She made a mental note to ask her next time they spoke. At the moment of her nostalgic thinking, the back of his hand lightly brushed hers, but she did not take hold of it.

He opened the front door and walked her to the living room. Three pledges sat up at attention on the couch, beanies on their heads, while the pledge master looked through their pledge books.

Johan said, "Oh, I forgot this was happening tonight. Let's go to my room." Annie slowed her steps and stiffened. "I'll keep the door open. I promise."

They entered his room, and it looked just as Annie remembered it, a mattress on a frame, rumpled sheets, chair at a desk, a couch along the wall, and a towel hanging from a nail. Something sat heavy in the pit of her stomach, and seeing the bed with the rumpled sheets made her stomach lurch. Johan led her to the couch.

"I'm glad you're here. I want to talk about us," he declared. "You're my girl, Annie. You're very important to me. I don't want to see anyone else." His words dripped from his lips like thick maple syrup from a honey dipper, smooth and slow.

Annie struggled with her disappointment in him, the belief that her dating life was over, and Johan was her consolation prize. She wondered if this was what she could live with, if her stained and damaged innocence could do no better than him. She decided to remain quiet and let him do all the talking. She really had no choice.

A part of her loved him, a part loathed him, and a bigger part feared him. She tried to hide her mental wrestling by smiling and listening. She shifted slightly on the couch as he took a seat in front of her on the distressed coffee table.

With his legs spread and bent at the knees, he rested an elbow on each thigh and took both her hands in his. "Annie, let's start over. Let's work on our friendship and pretend nothing ever happened." He looked directly into her eyes.

She held his gaze for a moment then looked beyond him to the oak tree outside the window. Its silhouette, outlined by a full moon, looked dark and ominous as well as intriguing. She kept her focus on the mystery beyond the window and wondered how many little sets of eyes were looking back at her. She heard Johan talking but didn't really pay attention to his words. Beyond the bedroom threshold, sounds of laughter and footsteps going up and down the stairs filtered into the room. Annie's shoulders relaxed as those intrusive sounds meant she was not alone with him. She maintained a hint of a smile on her face, her mask when she was experiencing something unpleasant.

In mid-sentence, Johan rose, walked to his turntable, picked out a Fleetwood album, and set the needle in the vinyl groove. "Would you like to dance?" He extended a hand to her. She rose slowly, being led more by the music than by his words or actions. She let him put his arm around her waist, but she would not let him pull her close. She was not ready for that. They moved to Stevie Nicks' "Landslide", Annie's favorite song.

They danced in the small space between the dark brown dresser and the bed. Annie kept her eyes open and avoided direct eye contact with him, by looking at the room around them. She decided that she would not kiss him, not tonight, not for a long time.

***

After the first side of the album ended, Johan flipped over to side two, and the dancing continued. He knew music was her passion. Next, he planned to play The Police. He located the album and took the vinyl out of its sleeve. He patiently waited as the first album finished and the automatic feature of the record player lifted the arm and robotically moved it to the needle rest. He placed the new album on the turntable, pressed a lever, and watched as the needle was gently set in the appropriate groove. With a bit of pre-show audio static, Sting's voice belted out, "Roxanne!"

Annie immediately reacted to the song by pulling away from him. She asserted, "No. No more music. I'm done dancing. It's getting late, I really should go back. You don't have to walk me home." She felt the front pocket of her shorts for her room key.

Johan, confused by Annie's behavior, stepped back and removed his hands from her. "What? Okay. We don't have to dance anymore. But you really don't have to go, yet. It's only 11:30." He turned toward his alarm clock and pointed at the red, glow-in-the-dark numbers on his digital clock, another gift from Annie.

***

"It's what?" Annie also looked at the clock. "Oh, no. I really didn't mean to stay out this late."

"What's the matter, Cinderella? Your stagecoach gonna turn into a pumpkin?" He laughed and took a seat on the couch. "Come on and sit. We'll leave in a moment."

Annie didn't smile at his silly joke but followed his request and sat beside him on the couch. Not looking at him, she spotted the beige telephone with its twenty-foot cord on his left nightstand. Both windows were open, and a cool breeze passed through the room, rustling the thin white curtains. Annie didn't know what she was going to tell her roommates when she returned home after them. The dance was scheduled to end at midnight, but the girls always passed up the after parties. "I really want to leave now."

"Okay. But I'm going to walk you home," he insisted.

"Okay. Let's go." Annie stood up and moved to the door. She stepped out of the room and encountered Luis in the hallway. She hoped she could slip past him without being noticed, but the hall was narrow, and he was at the top of the stairs she needed to take down.

"Hey, Annie. Did you go to the dance tonight?" Luis asked.

"No. I didn't, but Maddie and Christy did. It's good to see you." She hurried down the stairs, and Johan was close behind.

Once out of the house, Johan tried to hold her hand, but she kept both hands fisted in her pockets. Annie led the way up the road at a quick pace, and he had to lengthen his stride a few times to keep up. They walked in silence until they made it to Jesten Hall. At the entrance to the lobby, Annie stopped, turned to Johan, and said, "Okay. Thanks for walking me home."

"Sure. No problem. Will I see you this weekend?" he asked.

"I don't think so. I have a lot of homework," she said this, but it was the truth.

"Okay. Brunch on Monday?" he asked. The light behind Annie's head hid her face from him, so he could not see her frown.

"Maybe. Good night." She turned and walked into the lobby, past the front desk, and down the hall to the elevators.

***

Johan watched her walk away. He wasn't sure if things were good between them or not, and he didn't know why she reacted the way she did back at his house. Shrugging his shoulders and dismissing any negative thoughts, he turned and walked back home.

Chapter 14

Little Lies

Annie's trip to her room was undisturbed by any encounters with friends. She entered her room, kicked off her shoes, and sat on the edge of her bed. Chewing on a spot on her lower lip, she tried to sort out her conversation with Johan.

"He apologized to me for 'things that happened.' He said he loved me. He believes I am the only girl for him. . . My part in all this is that I do have feelings for him. But I feel very mixed up right now. I'm not ready to forgive him because he took something precious from me, and no one else is ever going to want me. He is the only one." It was this last thought that would seal the deal.

She breathed in deeply and let it out slowly. Then she rose from her bed, grabbed her pajamas and toiletries from her dresser, and began her bedtime routine. Before stepping into the shower, she checked her inner thighs. Her bruises had now changed to dark purple outlined in green. She was glad they were in a place where no one else could see them and wondered if all girls who were sexually active had the same bruises. She wished she knew someone she could ask.

The warm shower relaxed her and helped her clear her mind. There was no reason to worry about anything right now. She washed with her soft-scented shower gel, treating herself gently. However, she saved washing her hair for last as it was her favorite part. On her last trip to K-mart for her toiletries, she found a shampoo she used when she was in junior high. She didn't know what it was about "Gee, Your Hair Smells Terrific" shampoo, but the peppery, floral scent used to last in her hair all day. This smell brought back happy memories of skating at the roller rink and walking in socks to Pizza Hut afterward. She and her best friends, Michelle and

Debbie, also used the same shampoo. She giggled to herself as she wondered what Mr. Mosley, the social studies teacher, thought about all these girls and their smelly heads.

Just as she was turning off the shower, she heard Christy's and Maddie's voices in the bedroom. She was relieved she was in the shower, seeming like she had been home all evening. She dried off, slipped into her pajamas, wrapped her hair like a swami, and joined the girls in the room.

"Hi," Annie greeted them first.

"Hi," Christy responded. "You missed a fun dance. Lots of good music. The DJ knew how to keep us happy."

"I bet. Was Luis there?" Annie asked out of habit. She immediately regretted bringing him up because he saw her at the fraternity house.

"No. He had something to do with the pledges tonight. It's always a very secretive thing, so he never tells me what they're really up to," Christy offered.

Annie hoped that meant he would not spill the beans about her being at the house with Johan. She knew that neither Christy nor Maddie would approve. She was just going to have to keep this quiet.

"I'm going to shower next," Maddie chimed. "I had too much fun, and now I need to wash it off." She sniffed her pits, laughed, and disappeared into the bathroom.

"That girl," Christy said as she shook her head.

"Yeah. She's great," Annie added while putting her shower caddy away then removing the towel from her head to pat her hair dry. Taking her brush from her dresser, she began to gently brush tangles out from her long stands.

Christy commented, "Gee, your hair smells terrific." She laughed as she took a seat on her desk chair.

Annie laughed with her and plopped herself down on her bed. At first glance, it appeared like any other Friday night after a dance. Laughter, friendship, storytelling, were all the telltale signs of sorority sisters enjoying campus life. Annie planned on keeping her evening a secret.

Christy asked, "So what did you do tonight?"

"Aw, nothing. A little of this, a little of that. Nothing." Annie shrugged her shoulders and avoided any prolonged eye contact. She tried to mask her anxiety, but her right leg defied her as it took on a slightly nervous shake. She hoped Christy wouldn't notice.

"Well, I guess everyone needs a break from the world sometimes." Christy turned from Annie to slip off her shoes.

Annie's secret was safe with herself.

The Friday night ritual ended with all three girls lying in their beds in the dark, talking about dancing with boys they knew and ones they just met. As voices trailed off and the room became quiet, Annie stayed awake a little while longer, thinking about what she needed to do next. She considered preparing a dialogue to maintain control in a conversion and spent the next hour thinking about things she could say and how she could recite them in a way that wouldn't reveal if she was feeling afraid.

Chapter 15

Moving Forward

As the Spring semester blazed on, much time was spent on finishing papers, finalizing projects, and preparing for midterm exams. Christy and Maddie spent many afternoons and evenings away from their living quarters as they sought quiet places in the library to study or met with study teams.

Annie found herself at the fraternity house on multiple occasions when they were away. She tried to keep her girlfriends and her boyfriend away from each other. She wasn't sure how her friends would feel about the relationship, but no matter what they thought, she felt she had an obligation. There was no way around it because shame was the burden she wore like a cloak, and she believed it a journey she had to walk by herself. Wonderful as they were to her, she didn't think they would understand.

Annie maintained she had to try and fix the relationship, and her plan was to use communication and boundaries. For some reason, though, every time she took one step forward, Johan always said something to set her back.

On Thursday evening, while her roommates were away, Annie found herself sitting on Johan's worn couch. Dressed in lavender shorts, a short-sleeved white blouse, and tan sandals, she thought she looked cute and felt good about herself. This evening, she didn't plan to stay too long because she needed to tidy up her dorm room for the following night's ultimate study session.

Although she had her reading guides and novels with her to study for English, Johan insisted on cuddling. Annie gently shrugged away from him and said, "Johan, I really need to study."

"Aw, common. We can spend a little time smooching."

"Well. That's not what I'm here for."

"You really think you can get some studying done tonight?"

"Well, I was hoping. We can cuddle another time." She was beginning to feel uncomfortable, but she didn't want him to see her distress.

"Huh. Well, we can study now and maybe we can do something else later," he lowered his voice.

Something else later? She thought.

"You know, maybe you can spend the night." He looked at her and winked.

"Spend the night?'

"Yeah. It's time we take our relationship to another level. Look, girls have to do certain things for their boyfriends. That's just how it is," he insisted.

"What?" Annie couldn't tell if he was joking, but she had rehearsed what she would say if the topic ever came up.

"I'm just saying. We've been dating for a few months now, and I well . . . I was just thinking . . ." He leaned in to give her a kiss.

She pulled away and out came her prepared speech, "Wait. Let me see here. We hang out. We kiss. We go to parties. But never have you actually taken me on a date.

Everything is at someone else's expense, someone else's plan."

"Oh. You want to go on a date? Why didn't you say so?"

"Why do I have to come up with the idea?"

"Well, first. I don't have a job, and second, I don't have a car."

"You don't need a job and a car to ask a girl on a date. I feel like this is too easy for you. I'm here when you ask me to come. I meet you at school events. I have a part-time job and buy you things. What do you do for me?'

"Well. . ." he looked at her, blinked, then said, "I didn't know you wanted something more."

"Johan, I am sure you've had girlfriends before me. Didn't you take them out on dates?"

"Yeah, but I thought it was different with us. I thought we had passed all that."

"What? Really? Don't I deserve that, too?" Annie worried that she might have steered the conversation in a bad direction. She really needed to study and was not ready for a fight.

Johan paused, got up from the couch, and stood by his dresser. He looked around, drummed his fingers on the top then opened a small drawer. It was off its track, squealed, and opened at an angle. He shuffled through its contents, pushed photo negatives aside, and pulled out printed pictures. "Look. Here are things we've done." He held up several photos and began to name some events, "We went to the January Fest. We attended a formal. We danced at a "Love Hurts" party for Valentine's Day. See, we've done things." He spread the pictures like revealing his hand at a poker game.

"Johan, all those things were school functions. Your fraternity sponsored the January Fest and the Valentine's dance, and I paid for the tickets for the formal and dinner afterward. What have you done?" She looked up at him from her position on the couch and felt a bit worried that she might have just ruined the evening with the last question.

He pursed his lips, looked around the room, and returned his attention to her. "Okay. We'll go on a date."

"Really? Okay. When?"

"We'll go to a play, and I'll borrow someone's car to get us there."

"A play? I love that. Can we do it during Spring Break?" Annie felt some hope.

"We can't go during Spring Break; I'm going to be out of town. Hey. I saw a commercial for The Zach Theatre. I think they're showing *South Pacific*."

"Oh. You didn't tell me what you were doing for the break."

"Uh, yeah. Sorry. I'm going to the coast with the guys."

"No girlfriends are going?"

"No. Just the guys."

"Oh." Annie was feeling a bit left out. "Okay."

"So, do you want to go to the theater Saturday? It's an evening show."

"Yeah. Yes. I do. That sounds great."

Although Annie didn't like that he had made plans that didn't involve her, and that he had never thought about taking her on a date, she was grateful that the conversation had shifted from the idea of having sex. She knew this was a topic that couples had to discuss, yet she could not bring herself to consider it much less discuss it with him.

Annie thought that she should return to the dorms before the conversation morphed again, so she began loading her blue Adidas bag with her study materials. It was still early, and she could make it back to the dining hall before it closed.

Johan stood by the dresser, reorganizing the photographs before shoving them back into the drawer. "Leaving already?"

"Yeah. I'll see you Saturday."

"Not tomorrow?"

"No. I'm going to stay in and study on Friday so I can enjoy the show on Saturday."

"Okay. I'll pick you up at 6:00 pm."

"Okay." She slung her bag over her left shoulder, walked over to him, stood on her toes, and brushed his left cheek with her lips.

As she pulled away, he grinned with a gleam in his eye.

She quickly trotted down the stairs, left the house without acknowledging anyone on her way out, and hurried up the street.

Chapter 16

Working Out

Saturday morning's sunlight seeped through the window and warmed Annie's bed. The subtle change in temperature made her stir and reflexively slip her feet out from beneath her bear blanket, and arms followed suit as she worked to open her eyes. Her vision slowly focused after a few episodes of blinking and eye rubbing. She sat up and hung her legs over the side. Looking around the room, she remembered she was alone because Maddie and Christy had pulled all-nighters with their study groups. She yawned and shook her head to clear the sleep cobwebs from her mind.

As she arched her back and stretched, she noticed a slight pressure developing in her chest and a quickening in her heartbeat. She knew this feeling. It always sat dormant in her until the moment she committed to do something she didn't really want to do. *What's bothering me*? She wondered. Study guides and books sat on her desk, but she felt good about her Friday night study session. *Nope. That's not it.*

Spotting her tennis racket resting against the wall next to her desk, a strong need to exercise motivated her to get out of bed. She pulled her pink and white tennis outfit, sun visor, and matching tennis shoes from her closet then went about her morning routine, washing up and getting dressed. She grabbed her long hair and quickly braided it with ease, a simple habit developed a long time ago. In her reflection of the bathroom mirror, she noticed that the summer tan on her arms was fading. It had been a while since she had seen the court; too many events had interfered with her workout schedule. She pulled out the white wristbands from the mesh pocket of her blue Adidas bag and slipped them on. Finally, she grabbed her yellow and black tennis racket, twirled it in her right hand, and adjusted the main strings and the 18 cross string threads. The racket had been a Christmas gift from her brother, Tommy. She loved how he always knew what to get her.

Annie grabbed a beverage from the small refrigerator near her desk and stuffed it into her gym bag. Next, she slipped her ID and room keys into a side pocket and left the room. Once she was out of the dorm, she headed straight to the courts swinging her racquet arm to warm it up. She wasn't worried about having a partner as there were twelve courts to use. If they were all occupied, she was certain someone wouldn't mind if she joined them. That's how it was with tennis players; they were always ready and willing to play if a potential partner appeared. She found five courts on one side of the facility, filled by couples players, but the sixth court held one boy practicing his serve. She hurried over to him and asked, "Do you mind if I join you?"

The young man dressed in blue Ocean Pacific shorts and a blue and white striped polo, held his left arm in the ready to serve, with his racket in his right. He stopped and looked at her. "Oh, yeah. Sure."

She recognized him. He was that Derek boy from the dining hall, the one she met freshman year. His dishwater blond hair was slicked back from sweat or hair gel, Annie wasn't sure. His skin was the color of honey, quite the contrast of what remained of her medium tan. His blue-green eyes sparkled in the sun. She remembered those eyes from before, but today they were mesmerizing. She looked away from his gaze, hoping he couldn't read her mind.

The young man intercepted her thoughts, "Hi. I'm Derek. You're Annie, right? I remember seeing you practice out here last semester."

"Yes. You're Derek." she responded. Feeling like a dork for having repeated his name after he just told her, she mentally hit her forehead with the palm of her hand and felt herself blush.

"Yep. You want me to serve?" He held up the neon-green ball.

"Please." She flung her bag onto a side bench and hustled over to the other side of the net. She centered herself on the court and assumed the position to receive a serve. The match began.

Very little was said as they rallied. The ball easily jumped from one side of the net to the other like a pong on an Atari game. Derek whacked from his side, the ball bounced on her side, and she whacked it back. If spectators had been sitting on the sideline, their heads would have been moving left to right like a synchronized dance. As the morning marched on, the match went into a full hour. Their skills were even, making the game challenging for both. At 11:30, Derek's Swatch on his left wrist chimed. He hit the last ball and shouted, "Love all!" Neither player scored.

Out of breath with large droplets of sweat dripping down her forehead, Annie walked over to the bench. She grabbed her bag and rummaged past an empty canister, her Gatorade, and several loose tennis balls. "Sheesh," she whispered aloud, "I left my towel."

Derek unzipped his gym bag and pulled out two white terrycloth towels, handing one to her.

"Thank you." She dabbed her face and the back of her neck.

"That was a good game. Neither one of us scored. I've never had that happen before."

"Well, we didn't play that long. Why did you call the game? If we had gone on a little longer, I am sure I could have schooled you," Annie spoke as she pulled her drink from her bag. She and her sweat mustache smiled then chugged from her blue bottle.

"I was only planning on practicing for a few hours; I need to study for exams today. Don't you have tests coming up?"

"I do, but I studied last night. I also have work study hours to do today, so I'll study for four hours today." After wiping down her arms then dabbing at her face again, she held the towel out to return to Derek.

He shook his head and waved it off. "No. You can keep it."

"I'll wash it and get it back to you. What building do you hang out in?" She was more curious about his major than returning his towel.

"Oh. I'm in the business building most of the time. But there's no rush for the towel. What's your building?" He smiled as he busied himself with wiping himself off.

"Most of my classes are in the education building. I want to be a teacher." She didn't know why, but something inside of her wanted to impress him.

Derek nodded, stood, and picked up his bag. "Well, I'm headed back to the dorm. I think I want to shower before lunch. Hey, would you like to do lunch? My treat," he laughed.

"That would be nice, but actually, I have to get ready for work, and I'm all the way over at Jesten Hall. Where are you?" She tried not to sound too interested.

"Hey, I'm there, too! West wing, fifth floor." His eyes lit up as he flashed his bright smile.

"No. What? I'm tenth floor, same wing." She couldn't believe it.

"Well, then do you mind if I walk back with you?"

"No. Not at all."

This was a turn of events that Annie didn't anticipate. Here she was just minding her own business then she runs into someone who shares the same interests and lives in the same dorm. *Huh.* She thought.

They took the ten-minute walk back to their dormitory and talked about tennis, their courses, and dances. Once they reached their hall, Derek swiped his passkey and let Annie enter first. At the elevators, he pressed the cracked "up" button and waited for her to pass the threshold before he entered. She noticed all these gestures and found them endearing. These were things that Johan never did for her.

Once the elevator chugged to the fifth floor and the gray metal door slowly opened, Derek turned to Annie and said, "Well. This is my stop. Have a great day."

"Thanks. I'll get this back to you soon." She held up the towel.

He smiled again and exited the elevator. "Okay. See ya."

Annie returned the smile, pressed the button for the tenth floor, and the elevator chugged on. For a moment, she had forgotten about Johan.

***

Derek exited the elevator, took a few steps, then turned toward the closing doors. He wanted to ask her if she was seeing anyone. He wanted to spend more time with her. He thought she was sweet. Many thoughts were racing through his head, but one thought was certain. He wanted to see her again.

Chapter 17

Blindly Walking

Annie stepped out of the shower after a great morning of tennis. She took two blue towels from the shelf near the sink, wrapped herself in one, and secured her wet hair in the other. Her right thumb went directly to her mouth, and she chewed on her cuticle as she sat on her bed, pondering about what to wear. Nodding her head in agreement with herself, she decided to go to work already dressed for her date with Johan. Her shift would end at 5:30, and he was picking her up at 6:00. She walked over to her closet and considered her options. She pulled out a white, long-sleeved blouse with a sweet-heart collar. Next, she sorted through her four skirts: pencil, A-line, flared, wraparound, and narrowed it down to the red A-line and the blue wraparound. She held each one up to her physique and observed her image in the full-length mirror suspended from her closet door. Then she tossed the red one on her bed and hung the blue one up.

Her make-up routine was simple, a little rouge, lip gloss, and mascara. Done! The most challenging part of getting ready was drying and straightening her hair. With its length now nearing her waist, her hairdo options were limited. She decided to wrap it back up in a towel until she was fully dressed and let it dry in its naturally wavy state while she was at work.

She dressed and dabbed a bit of perfume behind each ear and on her wrists. Once her kitten pumps were on her feet, she unwrapped her hair, shook it out, and brushed it with her fingers. She filled her clutch purse with her dorm key, ID, and lip gloss. She was ready for her date.

Her shift at the front desk went smoothly. Door traffic was slow and the phone calls she had to answer had simple requests. This allowed her time to study, so she opened her green history spiral and read over her notes several times over the four hours. Before she knew it, her shift was over.

At 5:30, she placed her notes in a drawer with the intention to pick them up later in the evening when she returned. Annie thought about going back up to her room to put them away, but she wanted to be ready when Johan walked in to get her.

The clock on the front desk read 6:10. He was late. She stood by the glass doors and waited. At 6:15, a blue Buick pulled up to the curb and honked. This caught her attention, so she looked out. Johan stepped out of the driver's side and waved her over. *He can't even come in to get me?* She thought about turning around and walking away. Already the date was not going well. In the end, she stepped out of the building, descended the stairs, and let herself into the car.

"Hey. You look nice," he said as he sped away from the curb.

"Thank you." She wondered if she should ask about his tardiness, but she changed her mind. "Whose car is this?"

"It's Tristan's. He said he was staying in to study, so I could borrow it tonight. What do you think? It's nice, right?"

"It is." Something inside of her told her to walk around the evening on tiptoes.

Johan sniffed, pinched his nose, and licked his lips. Annie witnessed this and wondered what was going on with him because his left leg was also shaking. Then he said, "Hey. Well, we're going to the show, but we can't go out to eat because I don't have enough money."

"Didn't your parents send you your allowance?"

"Yeah. Well, I spent most of it already." He sniffled again. "Do you have any cash?"

"No. I didn't bring any money with me." This was the truth as she had spent her last paycheck on him. He had borrowed $50 and never paid her back. She thought better than to bring it up at the moment.

Johan drove on at a fast speed. He ran through yellow lights and frequently switched lanes for no reason as there was very little traffic. Annie clutched the armrest and remained quiet.

They arrived at the theater, with ten minutes until curtain call. The ticket booth was ready to close, and Johan sprinted over to it to get their passes. Annie watched as he stood at the window and flashed his charming smile at the attendant. He was dressed in a white cotton button-down, black slacks, and tan loafers with no socks. This struck Annie as strange as it seemed very casual for a production at this type of theater. Again, she decided not to make any comments.

"Okay. Here is yours. Let's go find our seats." He took her by the elbow and ushered her to the ticket taker. They found their seats just as the house lights went down and the audience began to applaud.

Johan sat with his legs spread apart. He placed both elbows on the armrests and clasped his hands together in his lap. Both his legs shook, and he fidgeted throughout the show.

Annie didn't know what to think about his behavior. She was hoping he would initiate hand holding, but he seemed to be in his own world. She decided to just enjoy the show.

At intermission, they stood near their seats and stretched. Because they didn't have any money, there was no reason to go into the lobby for a glass of wine or a small tray of cheese. Annie felt disappointed and feared that he could see it on her face. She hadn't eaten all day, and her stomach was having an animated conversation she was just sure everyone could hear. The thought of the cheese sticks and crackers in her refrigerator made her want the show to be over. She really wanted to go home.

"What do you think of the show," Johan asked.

"It's really good. I've always heard about it, and I'm glad I finally get to see it. I love seeing Gary Burghoff, from MASH in the show. He's very talented."

"Gary who?"

"You know, Radar."

"Oh, yeah. Radar. I didn't pay attention to which famous stars were in the show." He looked around at the crowd of people returning to their seats. "Oh, well. I guess it's time."

"Yes." Annie returned to her seat and patiently waited for the second act to begin.

Johan sat and took her small hand in his. Annie smiled at him, and the house lights went down. Although the second act on stage moved forward, the second act in the audience was more of the same. Johan's legs kept shaking, and he had the sniffles. He seemed very jumpy, and this made Annie feel uncomfortable. He let go of her hand halfway through the last hour and sat erect with hands shoved in his pockets.

After the show ended and the house lights went up, Johan abruptly stood and said, "Let's go."

"Do you want to get autographs from the cast?" Annie asked.

"No. Let's go." Johan turned and walked up the aisle. Annie hurried to keep up with him.

They maneuvered through the crowd and broke free near the entrance. Johan opened the oversized wooden doors of the playhouse and stepped outside leaving Annie to push the door herself.

"Hey. Why are we in a hurry?" she asked as she followed him into the parking lot.

"Well. The show is over, and it's time to go."

They arrived at the car, and Johan opened the driver's door and slipped behind the wheel. Annie opened her door and scooted into the seat. While reaching out to pull the door, Johan started the engine and placed it into drive. She barely had time for the door to shut before Johan pressed the gas. She clicked her seatbelt into place and held on to the arm rest.

"Johan, why are you in a hurry?"

"I'm not in a hurry. I'm just driving the car."

Annie didn't understand his urgency. She tried to read his facial features through the light beaming from oncoming cars, but it was frugal. She didn't know what to say nor what to do.

"I liked the play," she offered. "What did you think of it?"

"Eh. It was okay. A musical is a musical." He drove through a yellow light, and a yielding car honked at him. "What's your problem, dude!" he yelled at the other driver.

"Johan, you're going kind of fast." She felt she needed to say something in case he wasn't aware.

"No. I'm just driving. Get off my back."

The comment caught her breath in her throat. She uttered, "Get off your back?"

"Yeah. You're always ragging on me. First you don't want to give me more, then you want to go to a play, and now you're trying to control how I drive. What is it with you?

"What? Where is all this coming from? I thought we were getting along."

"You thought. . . You thought. . .You're always thinking," he jeered. "You know, you're not perfect. In fact, there is something very wrong with you. Sometimes I don't even know why I bother with you. I can have any girl I want. I wouldn't have to put up with your stupidity. You're stupid, and you don't even know you're stupid.

That's the worst kind of stupid anyone can be. I don't want to be with a stupid girl."

These words stung Annie all over. She was trapped inside a moving vehicle with a boy spewing ugly words at her, and she couldn't get away.

Johan drove through another yellow light, but the next light was red. Annie hoped he wouldn't run it. She held on tight. She knew the neighborhood as it was not far from her parent's home. When the Buick neared the intersection, Annie unclipped her seatbelt, and without giving it much thought quickly exited the car.

Johan watched her and yelled, "Get in the car. Get in the car, now!"

Annie climbed the sidewalk and yelled, "Go home, Johan. I don't need you to give me a ride." She walked away from the car and turned the corner to the right at the light. Her heels clicked a steady beat as she raised her head to face the road in front of her.

"Get in!" he yelled as he made the same right turn and followed her.

"No. Just go!" she hollered as she tried to hold back tears.

"Fine!" Johan sped the car down the road.

As he drove off, Annie slipped into the first alley she encountered. It was one she knew well; she and her best friends used to walk through it on their way home from high school. She trekked deeper into the passage, keeping to the soft grass, and leaning into the shadows. Back out on the road, the sound of tires squealing and a car racing down the street made its way past the large trees and trash cans that lined the alley. Annie knew it was Johan looking for her.

She walked for a mile, switching alleys, and zig-zagging her way to safety. She passed a neighbor's house and could see the children, sitting on the floor playing a card game. The mother was in the kitchen, finishing the dishes, and the father was at the dining table, reading the newspaper. The scene was peaceful and loving.

She made it to her parents' house and stood in the shadows of the mighty oak. Its branches swayed in a gentle breeze. The sweet-citrusy scent from the large white flowers that blossomed every Spring in the Magnolia tree filled the air around her. Under the moonlight, she could see the dark silhouettes of the massive trees in the front yard. A warm wave of comfort enveloped her. She was home.

The little bubble of peace that held her in the moment burst when she heard Johan's voice. The blue Buick was parked in front of the house, and the streetlights bouncing off the chrome bumpers looked cold and harsh. Her body shuddered.

At the front porch, Johan was saying goodbye to her mother. Annie caught the very tail end of their conversation.

"Thank you, Mrs. Cisneros," he said in a kind voice. To someone else, his words might have sounded sweet and sincere, but to her they were dripping with sticky tar. Fake words, fake feelings, fake man, made her stomach tighten.

Her mother replied, "Thank you for letting me know. Maybe she'll call me." Her voice was pleasant, but Annie could hear a tremor of worry.

Annie squatted behind the bushes that wildly grew underneath her bedroom window. Their branches stemmed out in different directions, catching and tugging on her hair. She watched Johan get into the car, slam the door, and quickly speed away from the curb. Annie waited.

Once the car was out of sight, she pulled away from the bushes and stepped into the ring of light that illuminated part of the sidewalk and the front porch. Her mother, dressed in a blue striped cotton dress and black house slippers, stood at the top of the steps with her arms crossed. Angelita turned to Annie.

"There you are. I think you have someone very worried," she said.

"Mommy," Annie whispered, her voice quivering.

"What is going on tonight? Johan was here looking for you. He said that you jumped out of the car." She tilted her head to the left and held out her arms to Annie.

Annie climbed the stairs and accepted her mother's embrace. "Mommy. It wasn't good. He was saying mean things to me, and I had to get out. I had to." What she had been holding in suddenly erupted into tears and a wave of emotion that first started in her stomach lurched into her chest.

"Come inside. Let me get you a glass of water." Holding an arm around Annie's waist, she walked her into the house. The living room light was on and reflected off picture frames honoring graduation moments, weddings, and elementary school. Annie spotted her toothless little seven-year-old self, donning a very short hair cut in one of the montages above the couch. She wrinkled her nose as she remembered that was the year she got head lice and shared it with her little sister, Julia.

Angelita led her to the dining table where the family shared many happy moments. Out of habit, Annie sat in the chair closest to the head of the table on the left side. That was always her spot. She watched as her mother grabbed a clear drinking glass from the drying rack, filled it with tap water, and gingerly brought it to her.

"Here you go. Now tell me what happened." Angelita took a seat at the head of the table next to Annie. She offered a small welcoming smile, and with eyebrows slightly elevated, her brown eyes held concern as she waited for her daughter to speak.

Annie sipped the water several times then shared, "We have had some problems, but I thought they were getting better. He borrowed a friend's car and took me to a play, but he drove like a maniac and couldn't sit still during the performance. When we got back in the car, he started driving fast again. I wanted him to slow down, but he just got angry and started calling me names. So I waited for him to stop at a red light, and I got out. I had to. I knew where we were, so I wasn't afraid to take the alleys."

Angelita sat quietly for a moment then affirmed Annie's choices. "You did the right thing, mijita. You got away from a possibly bad situation. Maybe you need to stay away from him for a while." Angelita reached across the corner of the table and held Annie's hand. She scanned Annie's face, smiled, and asked. "Have you eaten?"

"No. I haven't. Johan didn't have enough money to take us to dinner. How did you know?"

"You're my daughter. I know your hungry look. Let me fix you a plate. We had chicken mole with beans and rice tonight. Would you like that?" Angelita didn't wait for an answer; she rose from the table, pulled out a blue and yellow Talavera plate, and served generous portions from the three pots on the stove. Placing it on the counter, she rummaged inside a wire fruit basket near the sink and pulled out a ripened avocado with one hand while her other hand automatically reached into a small drawer and extracted a paring knife. With the ease of a master at her skill, Angelita sliced the avocado, punched out its pit, and scooped out the soft fleshy part. Arranging it on the plate, she quickly sliced the luscious green delicacy, and the dish was ready for consumption.

While she balanced it in her left hand, she opened a drawer with her right and extracted a spoon.

Annie watched in amazement at how coordinated, organized, and masterful her mother was in the kitchen. She had never noticed it before. She had always seen mealtime as a chore, never realizing that this was one of her mother's arts. Her admiration for her mother was abruptly interrupted by her stomach growling in several places at varying octaves. She was indeed hungry.

The dinner plate arrived with perfect timing. It was placed before her, and she automatically mixed the refried beans and Spanish rice together then infused them with mole sauce. She felt the reaction of her salivary glands pull along the sides of her mouth as she scooped her first bite with the spoon. The spicey, nutty flavors of the mole sauce, with hints of Hershey's chocolate, brought back so many memories of family sitting around the table, laughing, teasing. They were good thoughts that momentarily took her away from the potential danger she had just escaped.

Angelita returned to her chair, clasped her hands in her lap, and smiled as she watched Annie eating. "You always loved mixing all that together," she said as she formed a circle above Annie's plate with her index finger.

With her mouth full of food, Annie said, "It's the only way." She grinned at her mother with chipmunk cheeks. She knew that chicken mole was only made a few times a year in her home, and she felt fortunate that tonight it was on the menu. She savored every bite and took in its aroma, hoping to never forget it. Good feelings came flooding back to her and cleared her mind of some of the darkness that had been filling her with dread over the past month.

Encountering a few spicey places in her meal, she stopped to drink water and clear her palate. Then she looked at her mother and hoped that she could not see how rough things had gotten between her and Johan. A part of her wanted to open up and tell her mother everything, but the other part commanded she shouldn't.

Crickets outside the window began to chirp their evening serenade, and Annie leaned back in her chair. "Mommy, that was so delicious. I do miss your cooking."

Angelita smiled. "Well, thank you."

Annie returned her smile. She looked around the room and felt a short pang over the thought of leaving. She hated having to cut the visit short as this moment between them, with no other family member around, had never happened before. However, she knew that if she was going to walk back, she needed to start at that moment as the school was over two miles away. She inhaled the smells, the memories that accompanied them, and the love she felt radiating from her mother.

As she exhaled, she said, "It always feels good to be home, but . . . I have to get back. We have midterms coming up, and I want to be ready to study in the morning." Annie scooted her chair back and the familiar sound of the chair scraping against the hardwood floor made her smile. She scooped up her plate, spoon, and drinking glass and walked them to the kitchen sink, another routine she knew all too well.

"Mommy, I have to start walking back now unless you have the car tonight. If you do, do you think you can take me back to school?" Annie asked as she washed her dinnerware.

"I do have the car. I don't need it until Monday. I have a doctor's appointment in the afternoon. You can take the car, and come on Monday to pick me up. Will that be okay?"

"Oh, yes. That will work. Thank you, Mommy." Annie turned to her mother and gave her a hug. This time Annie noticed a hint of her mother's Wind Song perfume. She loved the smell of her mother.

Angelita received the hug and said, "Gee, your hair smells terrific."

They both laughed loudly, and the crickets outside momentarily stopped, then one at a time, resumed their courting ritual.

Angelita walked to the brown tree-hall that stood by the front door and retrieved her keys from her black purse and took them to Annie. She cupped Annie's hand in both of hers and said, "You be safe. Stay away from him, and I'll see you on Monday."

"Thank you," Annie whispered as she hugged her mother one last time.

Annie exited through the back door and located the brown station wagon parked in the driveway. Sliding onto the driver's side, she adjusted the seat, and started up the engine. The driveway, darkened by the shadows of the looming trees, was difficult to maneuver at night. She cautiously backed the car down the drive and carefully avoided running into the trash bins along the curb's edge. A sadness that she was avoiding showing her mother, spread across her face. It revealed itself in her reflection in the rearview mirror as she passed under streetlights. Slowly but incessantly, the heaviness of negative thoughts began to seep into her awareness, yet she drove on toward school, toward uncertainty.

***

Johan sped through the neighborhood of Annie's youth one last time. He had only been to her house once when she drove him there to meet her parents. He really surprised himself that he remembered where it was.

He grabbed a tissue from his pocket and wiped his runny nose. The high he started the evening with was beginning to wear off, and he thought it best just to head back to the fraternity house and call it a night. He had really hoped that Annie would have returned with him and that maybe she would have spent the night. After all, he had taken her on a date like she asked.

He cruised up and down the drag on Guadalupe Street. It was alive with college students enjoying one last weekend of freedom before midterms started. He thought about pulling over and grabbing a taco from a food stand on the corner, but he remembered he was broke. He had borrowed money for the play, and he was in a borrowed car. He continued his course in the direction of the university and to his unmade bed at the house.

After parking the car in the exact spot where he found it, he briskly ran up the porch steps and entered the living room. There was an impromptu party happening, and Johan willingly stepped into the next act of his evening.

There was a group of guys and girls sitting in a circle on the floor. A footlong blue bong was being passed between them. Johan joined the group and got himself in line for the next hit. He grabbed the lighter from the girl sitting next to him, put his lips over the mouthpiece, and quickly lit the bowl. With his first deep inhale, he felt the burn of the smoke spread through his lungs. Balancing the base in his hand, he handed it to the next person. Then he tilted his head back, formed a circle with his lips, and let the smoke out in rings. Puff, puff, puff, they rolled out and wavered in the air until the girl sitting next to him broke the smoke rings with her finger. He turned to her and recognized her glassy eyes and short curly hair. It was Tanya in a tube top and cutoff shorts, long white legs stretching out in front of her. He remembered those legs and how hot and heavy their relationship was before Annie came along.

Johan smiled at her, and she grinned back. Those luscious lips, those penetrating eyes caused a stirring inside him. He felt himself waking up at a level he hadn't experienced in a while. As the drug took over his thinking, he felt himself loosening his boundaries. A hungry desire pushed him toward Tanya. Thoughts of Annie were no longer. He wanted Tanya. He knew she could satisfy him as she never hesitated to give him what he wanted before.

The bong came back around to him, and this time he lit it, inhaled it, and blew the rings toward Tanya. She responded by slowly sucking them into her mouth.

His body felt calm and giddy at the same time. He was horny, a feeling he had been stuffing away for a few months.

Their hands touched as he passed her the bong, and she drank him in with her big blue eyes. He couldn't stop looking at her. She took her hit and softly blew it in his face.

This was the invitation. He could no longer control his urge. He winked at her then shifted his eyes in the direction of the stairs. He hoped she knew what it meant.

She winked back.

Breaking from her gaze, he took a deep breath and unsteadily rose from his position on the floor. "Thanks," he said to everyone and to no one at all. He left the living room and slowly mounted the stairs, hoping Tanya would notice.

At the top of the stairs, he knocked on Tristan's door.

"Come in," Tristan answered.

"Hey. Here are your keys. Thanks, brother," Johan tossed them to him.

"You're welcome. Did you have a good time?"

"Yeah. We did. Thanks."

Johan stepped away from the door accidentally leaving it slightly ajar. Then he turned to his own room, unlocked his door, and shut it behind him.

***

Tristan sat on his bed, studying for his psychology exams. He leaned over and placed the keys on a small yellow table next to his bed and returned to his studies.

Hearing a soft knock on the door across the hall, he looked up and saw a girl with short curly hair enter Johan's room.

"I don't understand him," he said to himself.

Tristan squinted, rubbed his eyes, and returned to his studies.

Chapter 18

Safe Zone

Annie drove into the university parking lot and parked the family station wagon in visitor parking. She got out and slammed the heavy door shut, carefully locking it with the keys, and took the well-lit sidewalk to the building. Her heels were the only ones clicking out a rhythm as she slowly marched up the stairs to the dormitory entrance. While she fumbled in her small purse for her passkey, someone opened the door.

Derek and Annie stood face-to-face at the entrance.

"Hey," he chortled.

"Hey," she chortled back. A butterfly did high kicks along the lining of her stomach.

"Did you have a good time tonight?" he asked.

"I did and I didn't, but that's a story for another day. I'm just coming back from my parent's house. I had a wonderful visit with my mother. She even lent me the car." She jingled the keys in front of him. "Until Monday," she giggled.

"That's nice. Are you parked out here?" He pointed to parking lot A.

"Yeah. It's the brown whale over there in visitor parking." She pointed and laughed.

"I am impressed. You can drive a big car." He snickered. "Well, I'm on my way out to pick up something edible. I don't know what, yet. Do you want to come along?" He extended his elbow as if to escort her down the stairs.

"You know, that is really sweet of you, but it's been a long day for me. But thank you for the invitation." She gave him a soft smile as she wondered why and how he could be such a gentleman. She felt she didn't deserve it.

"Well, okay. But I've asked you out to eat twice today. Maybe a third will be the charm." He flashed a confident smile that made her knees shake.

"Maybe," she said, trying to keep from sounding tickled. "Well, I hope you find something good. Goodnight."

"Thanks. Goodnight to you, too. I'll see you soon, Annie. . . Wait. What's your last name? I can't remember." He snapped his fingers, tapped his head with his keys, and pointed at her.

"Cisneros. I don't think I ever told you. That's why you can't remember." She smiled and shrugged her shoulders.

"Oh, Miss Annie Cisneros, I will see you soon." He slowly walked away then briskly descended the stairs.

Annie stepped into the building and turned to look out the glass door. As his image became smaller the closer he got to the parking lot, she realized that she was beginning to admire his carefree nature and his selflessness.

She turned to the front desk, walked around it, and reached for her history spiral. She wished the night watchman good night, then headed to the elevators.

The night moved on even though she was ready to end the day. Six students exited the elevator, smelling of a mixture of Polo cologne and Lauren perfume. They laughed with each other, hardly noticing her, and moved in a wave as they exited. Annie entered, pushed the button and took the lone ride up to the tenth floor. She was tired but knew that she needed just a little more energy to spend on her roommates.

She pushed her key into the lock, turned it, and was immediately greeted with the powerful smell of pepperoni pizza and parmesan cheese.

Maddie was standing by the door in her cotton nightgown, with a string of gooey mozzarella connecting her mouth to a slice of pizza.

"Mmmmm. Hey. Sorry, it's hot." She fanned her face in an attempt to cool the bite of pizza she had in her mouth.

"That looks good," Annie said as she hurried to her bed, dropped her purse and keys on the desk, and slipped off her shoes.

Christy, sitting on her bed, cross legged, fanned her hand over a large slice of pizza resting on a paper plate.

"Hey, Annie. I sure have missed you." Christy pointed to the box of steaming pizza on her desk. "You want some?"

"Thank you, but I ate at my parent's house," Annie reported. She avoided eye contact because she didn't want them to ask her anything. She knew she wasn't a good liar, and it was best if the conversation didn't go any deeper.

"It's been a tough, busy week. We've all been going in different directions. But midterms are next week, and then it's Spring break," Maddie sang. Her off-key vibrato made everyone laugh.

"Yeah! Spring break. I need this break really bad," Annie admitted as she took a pair of pajamas from her closet shelf, shook them out, and laid them on her bed. "You want to go to the evening mass tomorrow? I kind of need to get some good sleep in and then I have a few things to do before the day gets past me."

"Sure. I think that's a good idea. I'm going to get breakfast then I need to hit the library. What about you, Maddie?" Christy took a bite into her pizza.

"Yeah. I'm meeting with Tracy and Joanne to study one last time for psych class. So, I can go to mass in the evening."

It was settled. They would meet up again Sunday evening.

As her roommates finished their late-night dinner, Annie washed her face in the bathroom. She leaned into the mirror and inspected her facial skin, noting a few more freckles on her nose. She smiled then looked into her own eyes. Deep in the pool of chocolate brown, she could see shards of pain and shame. They stole the happy glow that was always a part of her and cast a mask of darkness across her face. She hoped no one else could see it.

Slipping into her pajamas, she hurried into her bed and snuggled herself between the sheets. Then she arranged the teddy bear blanket over her legs, pulled it up to her chin, and laid back. She listened to the chatter between her friends as her mind returned to the events of the evening. She needed to have closure. She felt she needed to check on Johan in the morning to make sure he was okay. She began to think that maybe he was not the person she was supposed to be with, that maybe she needed to free herself. As the voices in the room began to fade, it was becoming more difficult to keep her eyes open. Her thoughts peacefully floated and an image of a charming smile connected to beautiful hazel eyes that were like a mood ring changing from gray, blue to green drifted into view. She smiled back.

If Christy or Maddie had been watching Annie at that moment in her bed, they would have thought she was having a very happy dream.

Chapter 19

Close One

Annie was out of bed by 9:00. She showered, towel-dried her hair, and slipped on her Calvin Klein jeans, white tennis shoes, and lavender polo. She quietly moved around the room as Christy and Maddie slept. Her plan was to go to Johan and have a conversation about date night, but something inside her didn't feel very confident. She also noticed that just thinking about him made her uncomfortable. *It shouldn't feel this way if you love someone. Right?*

She grabbed her purse and car keys then looked around the room for anything else she might need. Shaking her head, she slipped out of the room and headed for the elevator. An odd hush hung heavy in the hallway like leftover ticker tape after a parade. There were no sounds of activity behind the dormitory doors, no microwaves buzzing, no overhead showers running. All the boisterous activities from the night before had been silenced. She had never realized how strange it was that dozens of people were all sleeping at the same time. As soon as she reached the elevators, she pressed the down button and elevator B opened. It was as if it was waiting for her. She entered an empty cart and shuttled her way down to the lobby.

As she exited the building, her left tennis shoe began making that dreadful nack, nack, nack sound of one that has encountered chewed, discarded gum. She stopped and looked at the bottom of her shoe. A sticky wad of green spearmint gum was partially stuck to her heel.

"Yuck! Who did this?" She grumbled as she searched the area for a stick. She limped over to the oleander bushes and mountain laurels that lined the lot. Finding a twig, she scraped the green sticky goo off her shoe. "At least it's on the edge. That's a lot easier to clean." It took several attempts, but it came off in one piece. She threw the stick back under the foliage and continued her trek across the parking lot.

As she mapped out her plan to drive to the fraternity house and speak to Johan, a strange gray cloud filled her head, and her pulse sounded in her ears, with a whooshing sound. She felt worry creeping its way into her chest, disrupting her breathing. *Nothing to worry about.* She thought. *We need to discuss what happened last night; it shouldn't be ignored.* She didn't quite have the practice dialogue in her head, but she was prepared to stand her ground if he should deny or dismiss the seriousness of his behavior.

It was 10:00 when she arrived at the fraternity house. The yard was littered with plastic cups and pizza boxes. Annie pushed trash with her foot as she walked up the sidewalk to the front do. There was no need to knock as the door was always wide open.

She stepped into the living room that smelled of stale cigarettes and spilled beer. Spots on the floor were sticky, so she stepped carefully around the room. As she ascended the stairs, she found loose change spotting the steps and a book of matches. Reaching the top, she turned to the right to knock on Johan's door. Something made her hesitate. She tried the doorknob, but it was locked which meant he was home. Annie crossed her arms in front of her and stared at the door.

Her thoughts were interrupted by the sound of the door behind her opening.

"Hey, Annie. I don't think Johan is home.

"Oh, but the door is locked.

"Yeah. I think he locked it before he left.

"Do you know where he went?

"No. Maybe he went to do laundry or something.

"Oh. Okay. Just let him know I came by, next time you see him. Okay?

"Yeah, sure.

"Thanks." Annie turned on her heels and sprinted down the stairs. She briskly walked over to the station wagon and sat behind the wheel before starting it. She didn't believe that he wasn't home. He was never one to get up early on Sunday if he didn't have to. But why would Tristan lie to her? She shook her head and for some reason felt relieved.

As she leaned forward to place the key in the ignition, something on the second floor caught her attention. She turned her head and looked upward. A girl from a different sorority, whose name she could not recall, was hurrying down the stairs. She jumped into a silver Fairmont and sped away.

As Annie slowly pulled away from the curb, she glanced up to Johan's window above the sidewalk and thought she saw the curtain move. She considered stopping and going back up to his room again, but something inside her told her to keep driving.

***

Johan was sitting on his couch when Tristan's and Annie's conversation filtered into the room. He glanced at his bed where Tanya sat lacing up her shoes. When Annie's footsteps down the stairs faded, he stood and unlocked the door.

"Hey. You've gotta go now," he commanded.

"What? Okay. Will I see you again?" Tanya asked, clutching her purse against her chest.

"No. Just leave through the balcony door." He held the door for her and shut it behind her when she stepped out.

He hurried over to the window facing the street and pushed the curtain aside. Below him was the Cisneros family car. He stepped away from the window, back teeth grinding. Holding both sides of his head between his hands, he paced the room. This situation could go in any direction. His thoughts vacillated. He could just move forward with Annie and apologize for whatever made her angry last night. Or she might find out about Tanya, and everything would be over. But if she never found out about Tanya, there would be nothing there to worry about. He just couldn't lose Annie. He wanted to own her, her body, her soul.

He decided to take a shower and call Annie when he was presentable.

Chapter 20

Gas Light

Annie returned to her empty dorm room and kicked off her shoes. She flung herself across her bed and lay on her side, facing Christy's bed. The blinking light of the desktop computer caught her attention, and she stared blankly at it as she tried to swim through the thick, soupy muck of her thoughts. She knew she had to plan a conversion with him. She knew she couldn't just ignore his behavior. She knew something was wrong this morning but couldn't put her finger on it.

Her thumb immediately connected with her mouth, and she began chewing her cuticle. Since nothing clear was coming to her, she closed her eyes to block out visual distractions in the room. She breathed deeply and tried to relax. After five minutes, the best she could do was lie quietly on the bed. She straightened her position and placed her head on the pillow. "May as well take a little nap," she whispered.

The peal of the phone ringing caused her to jolt up. She felt confused for a moment about where she was and the time of day and searched the room for some way to orient herself. The sun outside the window was high and bright, causing Annie to squint as she rose from the bed. She made it to the phone by the fifth ring.

"Hello?"

"Annie? This is Johan," his voice was steady and firm.

"Oh. Hello. I went by to see you this morning. Wait. What time is it?" She turned around to look at her clock.

"It's 11:30. Sorry I missed you. How are you?"

"I'm fine. I went by to talk to you about last night." She steered directly to the necessary topic. "It didn't go as I had hoped."

"No. It didn't. You jumped out of the car."

"No. I got out at a light. You were driving recklessly. I didn't like it. I didn't feel safe. I kept asking you to slow down."

"There was nothing wrong with my driving. You just scare easy. You're always like that. You always overreact. You're doing that now." He paused for a moment then added, "Look. I didn't call to argue. I just wanted to see how you were doing and if you wanted to meet for lunch."

Annie's jaw dropped. She couldn't believe how he was dismissing his part in last night's disaster of a first real date. Her eyes darted from one spot in the room to another as she searched for the right words to say that wouldn't cause him to explode.

"I don't want to argue either, but I can't ignore how things turned out last night."

"Well, the way I see it, you got crazy, jumped out of the car, and ran off somewhere. I looked for you and couldn't find you, so I went home."

"Wait. You looked for me then you just gave up? You just let me walk in the dark all the way back to the dorm, and you didn't even check on me later to see if I got back?" Annie knew the truth about his visit to her mother, but she didn't want to reveal this to him. She stood in her room with one hand on her hip and the phone to her ear. She wanted to just hang up and never speak to him again. But guilt and shame still nagged, reminding her of his threat. She needed to walk around him carefully.

"Well, I'm checking on you now."

"You're checking on me now. Huh. Well, right now, I just need to be by myself. I have a lot to think about."

"What? Are you breaking up with me?"

"I said I have a lot to think about. We have exams next week and then we have Spring break the week after. I need time to myself."

"No. I'm not ready to end anything. I'll give you time, but we will talk." He paused again. "I love you, Annie. I've told you that. I want you."

"Johan, I need to go." She could have stayed on the phone all afternoon if the conversation hadn't turned into a gaslighting event. When he didn't respond, she hung up the phone.

Chapter 21

Sunday Blessings

Annie spent the rest of Sunday afternoon studying for her first midterm. Although she felt confident that she knew her literature well, she thought it wouldn't hurt to review her notes one more time. The test was going to be a combination of multiple choice and open-ended questions, and she thought she was ready.

She decided to take a break before her roommates returned, so she reached for the radio on her desk and turned it on. Then she stretched out on her bed and stared up, mindlessly watching the blades of the ceiling fan rotate. She caught the tail end of Casey Kasem's top forty and smiled at his familiar voice. The Car's "Drive" started up, and for the first time, Annie listened to the lyrics. The clear words of "You can't go on, thinking nothing's wrong" spoke loudly to her. The sad melody reached deep inside her and turned every emotion she had tucked in and put away completely upside down and inside out. It scattered her feelings in every direction and started a parade of tears to spill over her lashes. She realized that the relationship truly was not healthy, but she didn't know if she had the strength to fix it. She was starting to think that she might just have to live with the consequences of what walking away might bring. She didn't know who to talk to. Other than her two friends, who would believe her or support her in her decisions?

Annie let it all out. She let herself ugly cry and thrash around on her bed. The guilt and shame that burdened her were writhing their way out in a heaping mangled mess. She couldn't hold them back. She cried for every part of her that he hurt. She cried for the part of her that deserved better. She rose from the bed for a tissue and held her throbbing head. Heavy sobs and runny noses always came with a dreadful side of headache.

She walked into the bathroom, switched on the light, and examined her reflection. The words *I'm beautiful, I'm smart, I'm worthy* popped into her head. These were old words from her childhood that always helped her reset herself when someone had treated her badly. She spoke them out loud, "I am a beautiful person. I am intelligent. I am deserving, and no one can take that away from me." She hadn't thought about herself in such a way the whole semester, but now she knew she had to turn it around. She had to.

She grabbed a clean washcloth from the shelf and ran it under cold water. Wringing it out, she then placed it over her eyes to lessen the swelling. Her tear-stained eyes and red nose were going to be difficult to hide from her roomies, but she thought she might be able to make them look less obvious. Running the towel under the faucet one more time, she wrung it out and placed it over her forehead as she walked back to her bed. She lay on her bed and closed her eyes. Splotches of reds, greens, and blues appeared in her imagination. They grew and faded away then morphed into pastels. She was calming down, finding peace.

At four o'clock, Maddie walked into the room. "Hey. Oh. Is everything okay?" She walked to Annie and sat on her bed.

"Yes. I just have a headache. It's not a big deal." Annie didn't want to say anything about her cathartic experience just yet.

"It has been one of those days." Maddie patted Annie's leg then walked into the bathroom and shut the door behind her.

Like clockwork, Christy entered and walked directly to her own bed. She sat and looked at Annie. "Are you okay to go with us tonight?"

"Yeah. I'm okay. I really do want to go to church. I always feel so good when we're there and then afterward."

"Yeah. Me, too"

"Me, too!" Maddie yelled from the bathroom.

Annie and Christy broke out into heavy laughter. Christy accidentally snorted, and Annie's laugh turned into deep belly guffaws lasting the whole time that Maddie was indisposed.

The toilet flushed and the faucet ran for 20 seconds. There was a momentary pause then the bathroom door opened. "What's so funny?" Maddie looked from one friend to the other.

"You!" Both girls exclaimed.

Like something familiar and routine, the girls gathered their purses and room keys. They left their dorm room and made their way to elevator A. Annie checked her coin purse to make sure she had her Sunday offering. She did. The elevator opened, and they joined six other passengers. On its voyage down, the elevator stopped on the 5th floor, and the door shimmied open at the same time as elevator B door. Annie was busy sorting through the change in her purse and only caught a glimpse of two pairs of blue jeans-covered legs moving toward the second elevator and disappearing. Her door shut, and the cart continued its descent, stopping two more times on its way to the ground floor.

At the end of the journey, eleven people exited with her. Three went to the dining hall, and the other seven walked down the sidewalk toward church.

A cool spring breeze picked up, teasing everyone's hair as it filtered past them. Two girls in the group were chatting about midterm exams. The rest of the group strolled down the sidewalk in silence.

Entering the small church, the Beta Epsilon Lambdas marked themselves with the sign of the cross and joined two other sorority sisters already seated in a row of pews to the right of the altar. They always sat at the end of the pew near the back of the church. It had been Annie's suggestion to sit in this particular spot. Her argument was that you never know who is in church with you if you sit in the front.

Annie smiled as she felt herself relaxing and able to listen to the readings. The last few Sundays, while sitting through the liturgy, she had been very distracted with problem solving and missed some of the lessons completely. Tonight, she was open to receiving. She felt freed from something that had been binding her.

When communion began, Annie decided she would go up for a blessing. She hadn't been to confession in a while, so a blessing was the best she could do. She rose from her seat and walked up the aisle with her head held high and her arms crossed over her chest. Although she knew she shouldn't, she couldn't help but scan the pews ahead of her as she walked forward.

The communion line in front of her was long, so she could watch people returning to their seats. Trying to keep reverent was becoming difficult. She kept searching for familiar faces. She didn't really know why; she just was. A boy in a pair of blue jeans and a black, yellow plaid shirt caught her eye. She watched him return to his seat, cross himself, and kneel in prayer. As the communion line moved her to the end of his pew, she glanced at his face, and it caught her breath. It was Derek. She didn't know he was Catholic. Something in her chest fluttered, and she averted her eyes, hoping he didn't notice her looking at him.

After receiving her blessing, she walked down the right side of the pews to return to her seat. She passed Derek who was wedged between three of his fraternity brothers and two girls from a sister sorority. He had his hands clasped and his eyes closed in prayer. She hoped that he had seen her. She wanted to be seen.

Returning to her place next to Christy. She knelt for a quick prayer then stood with the congregation for the benediction. Mass was over, and she felt refreshed and renewed.

The church bells rang as students filed through the threshold of the big wooden doors. Multiple conversations with varying degrees of energy started up in different places in the crowd and spread like wildfire. Students sounded happy; some were singing. Annie looked around the crowd to see if she could spot Derek. She located some of his fraternity brothers, but he was not among them.

Assuming that he had left, she turned to Christy and Maddie and found Derek walking toward them. She tried to hide this new feeling that was racing through her.

"Hello, ladies," Derek greeted.

"Hey," Christy replied. "How are you, Derek?"

"I'm well. How are you?"

"We're fine," Maddie piped in.

"Hi," Annie said, trying to hide her surprise. "Derek, these are my roommates, Christy and Maddie."

"Oh. You all live together. Then can I escort you all back to the dorm?" He asked.

"Sure. We are headed to dinner. Have you eaten?" Christy waved her hand toward the

university.

"I have not. Would you like to join me for dinner?" He smiled.

Annie said, "Yes. That would be great."

Everyone nodded their heads in agreement and began their travels up the sidewalk.

Without anyone planning it, they paired up, Christy with Maddie and Annie with Derek.

Derek whispered, "The third is the charm."

Annie chuckled, "Yes. It is."

They walked among the mob of students heading to the same place. Entering the dining hall, Maddie rushed to find a table for four, while the others stood in different lines of various cuisines. Annie went to noodles and pasta sauce, Christy to Cajun and creole spices, and Derek to the ocean fried and grilled. They waved to each other as they waited their turns.

Tristan stood behind the counter and smiled, ready to serve Annie. "How may I help you?" he asked as he held a plate and spatula ready.

"Oh, hi, Tristan. I think I will have some lasagna and a side salad tonight. Thank you."

"Excellent choice," he said in his muddled accent.

Annie smiled, took her dish and placed it on her tray. She moved down the line and gathered her silverware and a plastic cup of water. Finding Maddie at a table near the windows, she placed her tray down and said, "Your turn."

Without hesitation, Maddie moved to a line with fried rice and lemon chicken.

Derek joined Annie with his tray and sat across from her. "It's good to see you again. Are you ready for next week?"

"Yeah. I think I am."

"I sure would like to play tennis again with you when this week is all over. Are you going anywhere for Spring Break?'

"Actually, I'm going home. I probably won't leave until Saturday."

"Ah, I'm going to the coast with some of the guys. Maybe we can play when I get back."

"That would be nice." She unraveled her silverware, laid the napkin on her lap, and placed her utensils on her tray.

Christy joined them at the table and set her tray down on Annie's right. She scooted into her seat just as Maddie walked up. When everyone was seated, Christy led the group in a blessing. After signs of the cross were made all around, a lighthearted conversation of cuisine, exam stress, and spring break plans consumed the dinner hour.

Annie felt happy, a happiness that was emerging from a dark web of gloom and sorrow. Inside her stomach, the butterflies became a rabble for a moment, but this was a good thing.

Chapter 22

The Distributor

On the first afternoon of midterm exams, Tristan crouched in the oleander bushes on the far side of the Jesten tower parking lot. Two pledges squatted with him. They waited to see whose car they had pulled the distributor cap from. *What a funny prank,* he thought. Then he spotted her. Annie, dressed in blue-jean shorts, a blue sorority shirt, and a pair of white sandals, walked over to her brown Mercury station wagon, unlocked it, and slid inside.

What started out as a joke began to feel very wrong. He heard her attempts to get the engine to turn over and watched her face grimace with every try. Although the wind blew frequently and disturbed the branches around him, they did not obstruct his view. He saw her get out of the car, lift the hood, and peer around.

He didn't feel right. This was no longer a prank. She had somewhere to go, and his actions were preventing it. He struggled with stepping out and stopping the prank or staying loyal to a fraternity brother. Her soft voice interrupted the wrestling match in his mind.

"Oh, no. What should I do? I've gotta pick up Mom." Annie stood at the side of her car, gripping the keys in her hands. Then she turned toward the building, climbed the concrete stairs leading from the parking lot to the ground-level patio outside of the dormitory, and walked inside.

Tristan suspected she was heading back to her dorm room. He watched her until she was out of sight then crawled out from the bush, shaking pink petals of the oleander blossoms onto the dark mulch underneath.

He called out, "Hey, Johan!"

In a loud whisper, Johan answered, "What?"

"Hey, man. This isn't cool. I didn't know we were doing this to Annie. I thought we were playing a joke on someone from another fraternity, a Sigma or a Kappa Sig. I've got two of my pledges here, and now I've got them involved in something that's not right."

"Fine. You guys can go. Just give me the cap. I'll deal with it." Johan extended his hand.

Tristan tightened his grip on the cap in his right hand. He placed his left hand in his pocket. Struggling again with loyalty to his fraternity brother and a strong sense that something did not feel right about this prank, he shook his head and replied, "I'll just wait for this to be over." He returned to the oleander bush where his captive audience of two guys in beanies lurked, anticipating their next order of duty.

"Hey, guys. Just wait with me for a while. I'll need you to help me put this back on," he whispered.

They responded in a hushed, "Sir, yes, Sir."

Ten minutes had passed since Annie had returned to the dorm. Tristan felt a cramp developing in his quads. He was debating whether he should just stand up, when he spotted Annie coming down the concrete stairs. She returned to her car with its lifted hood, peered in, wiggled a cable or two, then slipped back behind the wheel. She turned the ignition, only to hear a click and single chug from the engine. She got out of the car, slammed the door, removed the metal prop bar, and let the heavy hood drop.

Then a roaring laughter exploded from behind the shoulder-high hedge, and Johan stepped out. "Where do you think you're going?"

Tristan watched from behind the blossoms and narrow leaves but didn't know what to do.

Annie's voice came back thick and forceful, "Johan, what are you doing here?"

"Nothing. Just wondering how you're going anywhere if your car doesn't work," Johan shouted.

Tristan felt the energy in the air turn toxic as the hair on the back of his neck stood at attention. He observed the fight-or-flight situation he had read about in psychology develop right before his eyes.

"How did you know my car wasn't going to work? How is it that you're here at this very moment?" Annie's voice raised an octave.

"Well, I told you I didn't want you going anywhere today." Johan moved slowly toward her.

"What? I have to take my mother to the doctor. This is the only car we have." Annie's voice cracked.

"Well, I guess she's just going to have to ride the bus. You may as well call her and tell her you can't take her."

"What? Do . . . Do you have something to do with this?" Annie pointed to the car.

"Maybe."

"Johan, what did you do? I have to go. My mother needs me, and I have to return the car."

"No."

"Johan! Please!"

"No."

"Damn, you!" Annie screamed.

Johan smiled, "I'm not doing anything."

"You will or I'll get security."

"And tell them what? I haven't done anything to your car."

"Yes, you have. I don't know what, but yes, you have! I can't believe you are being such an ass!" Annie's cheeks turned red, and her nostrils flared.

"If I'm an ass then you're a psycho! You should go get therapy for yourself because you're crazy."

"What did you do to my car?"

Tristan couldn't stand the confrontation anymore. He looked at the distributor cap in his hand and realized that he had been set up. Although it was true that he hadn't touched the car, Johan was still very much involved as he had instigated the situation. What Tristan thought was a prank was truly an abusive act. He saw that perhaps Johan wanted to hurt Annie without leaving fingerprints, and he decided he didn't want to be a part of it, any of it.

He chose to stand up for Annie, and he stepped out from behind the bushes. He turned to the pledges and said, "You guys come out with me. Right now, for this very moment, you are not pledges. We are three guys who are going to right a wrong." With that, all three men stood and stepped out onto the pavement.

"Annie," Tristan softly called.

She jumped at the sight of three men emerging from the shadows. Tristan witnessed her tear-filled-eyes glisten in the sunlight as she stood with her legs slightly apart, knees slightly bent and thigh muscles flexing. He glanced at her right hand that firmly gripped the car keys. Three keys protruded between each finger, forming a makeshift weapon. Her eyes darted from one man to the other. He sensed her fear as he observed the flesh on her knuckles turn white and the muscles of her jaw tense.

"Annie, it's okay… It's okay… I'm not going to hurt you." He held his arms down by his side. "I have your distributor cap. Look. Here." He extended his right hand to show her while he used his peripheral vision to keep an eye out for any sudden moves from Johan. He was beginning to wonder about Johan and whether he was a good guy.

"Tristan, no wait! What are you doing?" Johan yelled.

"I'm giving it back to her," Tristan responded. He took a step toward Annie and said, "Annie, this is what is keeping your car from starting. I'm really sorry. Johan asked me to remove the cap from a car, but I didn't know it was your car. I'm really sorry, Annie. Really." He held out his left hand, palm out like a mime who was stopping a wall from closing in. "Can we put it back?" He stood with one foot forward, left hand out, right hand holding the cap.

Annie stayed tense and curtly answered, "Yes."

With her consent, he and the two fledglings hurried to the car, raised the hood, and went to work at returning what they had taken.

Johan watched, with hands on his hips and feet firmly planted.

"How could you do this to me? How is this a way to treat someone you are supposed to love?" Annie yelled, her voice loud and forceful.

"I thought it would be funny." Johan shrugged his shoulders and grinned.

"Were you ever going to put it back so I could drive the car?"

"Eventually."

"Eventually?"

Tristan couldn't ignore the words between the two. He was mentally preparing himself to have to physically stop any stupid move Johan might make toward Annie. She was a sweet girl, and he was starting to realize there was something very wrong with his fraternity brother. Very wrong. Once the task was completed, he turned from the car to face Johan and decided to stay near until Annie left.

Annie slid behind the wheel and started the engine. After backing out of the parking space, she quickly shifted into drive and sped out the exit into traffic.

Johan stepped out from under the shade and approached Tristan. "Hey. What'd you do that for? I was going to give it back."

"It wasn't right, Johan. It wasn't." Tristan looked away from Johan to gather himself. He was repulsed by his brother's behavior and attitude. Turning to the pledges he said, "Let's go guys. This is over. You did the right thing." The three walked away from the scene of the crime and filed into Tristan's Buick. The engine rumbled as they drove out of the lot. In the rear-view mirror he watched Johan place his hands in his pockets and turn in the direction of the cafeteria.

Chapter 23

Book Scrap

Saturday morning rolled in and turned into afternoon before Annie stirred in her bed. Since the Monday incident, Johan never called to apologize and never attempted to see her. Normally she would have been upset about the lack of contact, but she felt relieved. She didn't need anything to distract her from her exams. It was an exhausting week, and she was ready to go home.

Since Christy and Maddie had left on Friday night, that left Annie alone to sleep in and wake up at her own pace. When she finally rolled out of bed, the sun had already shifted to its 2:00 position. She wasn't very hungry, so she thought she'd skip the dining hall. She wasn't concerned about packing as she still had multiple changes of clothing at home. She rose and walked into the bathroom, washed her face, and brushed her teeth. She considered not taking her toothbrush but changed her mind when she remembered a time her brother, Adrian, used her brush to clean his comb. *Yuck. I better take this just in case he's living at home.* She wanted to beat him up that day, but she was so appalled and disgusted, she chose to stay away and let her mother handle him.

She decided to change the sheets so she could come back to a clean bed. Then she disrobed and placed her dirty laundry in a hamper under her desk. From her closet, she pulled out a pair of lavender Ocean Pacific shorts and a white button-down blouse adorned with green leaves and lavender flowers. Clean underwear and a pair of balled up white crew socks were retrieved from her chest of drawers. She dressed then spritzed herself with some Jean Nate perfume.

She took her gray backpack and stuffed the large compartment with a few novels, her toiletries, and finally her purse. As she went about checking other pockets, she encountered some money and an olive green Scrunchie. She swiftly took the hair tie and swooped her long strands into a thick ponytail. Then she sat on her bed, laced up her tennis shoes, stood, and hoisted her backpack over her shoulders. She was ready for a three-mile hike home. With her keys in her hand, she looked around the room one last time, shrugged her shoulders, and stepped into the hall, gently closing the door behind her.

The hallway was quiet, but she could hear the elevator at the end of the corridor still running. As soon as she reached the elevator, she pressed the down button and looked up at the floor location indicators, wondering what level it was coming from. The bell dinged and the door slid open. In the distance a phone rang. She turned her head to look down the hall in the direction of her room and wondered if it was hers. Shaking her head as she entered the empty elevator, she decided that it didn't matter. She grasped the straps of her backpack with each hand as she descended. What she needed was waiting at home.

Out on the road, Annie kept to the sidewalks as she made her way back home. She knew these streets well; she had walked them every day during her freshman year before she moved to the dorms. Taking a deep breath and smiling, she entered the parking lot of a 7-Eleven and reached to the side pocket of her backpack to rummage for loose change. As if on autopilot, she walked directly to the 1970s soda machine, its red lettering on white background fading from years of sitting in the sun. The coins rolled into the slot, and she waited for the click that signaled her to open the side door and pull out a bottle. It was the easiest test she had taken all week. She had a choice between A. Orange Nehi, B. Grape Nehi, or C. Royal Crown Cola.

She pulled the door open and withdrew her favorite. Quickly positioning the cap in the bottle opener on the side of the machine, she popped it off. With the fizzy grape happiness at her lips, the distinct sweet smell that made her think of the color purple, the fusion of acid and syrup, and the clean, cold smoothness of the glass bottle in her hand brought back memories of summer fun with her sister, Julia. They would save up found change and any money they had earned to visit the store to get soda pop and bubble gum. Sometimes, if they were lucky, they had enough to split a candy bar.

Annie's steps became lighter and quicker as she drank her liquid confection and found herself down the street from her family home. She could see the different shades of green in the treetops and the white blossoms bursting open on the two big trees that stood on each side of the porch. The fruity, champagne fragrance of the magnolia blossoms always made her feel good.

Reaching the front yard, she bound up its small hill, sprang up the steps, and knocked on the door.

"Come in!" her mother hollered from the kitchen.

Annie opened the screen door, entered the house, and out of habit, dropped her backpack by the door. "Hi, Mommy. It's me."

Her eleven-year-old brother, Mateo, was sitting on the couch watching MTV videos on cable and turned his head when he heard her voice.

"Hey, Mattie. How are you?"

"Hey, Annie. Are you home for Spring Break?" Dressed in baby blue pajamas and white socks, he jumped up from his seat and hurried to hug her. He put his arms around her waist and lifted her two inches off the floor. Putting her back down, he proclaimed, "Look, I'm getting stronger. And look, I'm getting taller." He took his right hand, placed it on his head, and tried to measure his height against hers.

"Yep. I'm staying for a few days. And yeah. Look at that. You are getting taller," she giggled and ruffled the light brown hair on top of his head.

"Great. Maybe we can make some Jiffy Pop and watch a movie tonight."

"That will be great, Mattie. Where's Mommy?" She looked around from the living room to the dining room.

"She's in the kitchen." Mateo pointed to the kitchen. He grinned at his sister, nodded his head in agreement, and returned to his show.

"Of, course," Annie smirked and walked to the kitchen and leaned against the door frame. She crossed her arms and quietly watched her mother pounding meat with a tenderizer.

Angelita looked up at her daughter and said, "Ay, mijita. You're here." She stopped her work and crossed the room to give her daughter a big hug.

Annie placed her soda pop bottle on the counter, took her mother in her arms, closed her eyes, and felt safe, safer than she had felt in a long time.

"Hi, Mommy. What can I do to help you?" Annie pulled away and looked around the kitchen.

"Oh, you can come back later when I am ready for breading and frying. I am making one of your favorites, milanesa." Angelita winked.

"Oh, wow! I should come home more often. First mole and now milanesa." Annie clasped her hands over her heart. "I feel so special."

"Well, you are. Now go see your sister. She cleaned up the room for your visit." Angelita took Annie by the shoulder, turned her around, and pushed her toward Julia's bedroom.

Annie walked through the living room and down the hall to the room she had shared all her life with her sister. There were stickers on the door that read, *Stay Out, Enter at Your Own Risk,* and a homemade sign on notebook paper that read *Brothers Not Allowed!* She knocked.

"If you're a boy, you can't come in," yelled a voice from the other side of the door.

Annie opened the door and poked her head in. "Well, I'm not one, so I guess I can come in."

"Annie! When did you get here?" Julia jumped off her bed and ran to hug her big sister. Although there were several years between them, Julia, with her curly auburn hair, was already an inch or two taller than her big sister.

The two sisters stood between the two twin beds in their room and hugged like it had been years since they had seen each other.

"Hey. I'm home for Spring Break. What are you up to?"

"Well, I have soccer practice today, but I'll be home later tonight. Maybe we can do something."

"If you want to watch a scary movie and eat popcorn, then you have a date. I already promised Matt that I would stay in tonight."

"That's great. I'll make sure to come straight home after practice. In fact, it's almost four, I have to leave in a few minutes. Misty is going to pick me up." She turned her wrist and looked at her watch. "She's probably on her way now."

"Hey. That's okay. You don't have to cater to me. I'll see you when you get home." Annie sat on her bed and bounced as she watched Julia get her gear together. "I'm going to help Mommy with dinner in a little while. I'll make sure to save some milanesa for you."

Julia wrinkled her nose and shook her head. "Make sure that my piece doesn't have any onion or bell pepper on it. I hate them."

"Will do." Annie laid back on her bed and tucked her hands behind her head. Outside the bedroom window a Jeep honked.

"Well. That's my ride. I'll see you in a few hours, sis." Julia took her blue and red gym bag and slung it over her shoulder.

"Okay. I'll be here." Annie waved to her as Julia hurried out the door.

Annie looked around the room from her place on the bed and saw how Julia had taken it over. Smelly socks were strewn in different places on the floor, the clothes hamper was overflowing, and dingy gray shin guards were on the nightstand next to the yellow telephone. The only place that appeared organized was the small bookshelf in the corner. Julia's books were always organized.

After Julia left, Annie moved to the floor and reached for a large white box under her bed. She removed the lid and scoured over a pile of loose photographs. Sorority pictures, even the private ones, and party scenes stared back at her. Over Christmas break, she started a photo album. She liked putting events in chronological order then arranging pictures in a linear sequential manner. Photos were lined up, much like paintings in an art museum. Each picture was just as important as the other, and since her camera was an inconsistent two-dollar bit she bought at a garage sale, a whole roll of film hesitantly produced a handful of useful negatives. At most, she had six good pictures per social event. She peeled back the magnetic plastic cover of a photo album page and exposed the glue-streaked cardboard where she placed her pictures. Picking up where she left off at Christmas, she wrote the date on a small strip of notebook paper, to mark the historical event, and pressed it onto the sheet.

This picture was of her and Johan at a fraternity party. She wore her purple and black striped dress, and he had his arms around her. He looked happy, but she could see a darkness in her own expression. His eyes were glazed from overindulging in alcoholic libations and neither eye was focused in the same direction. Her eyes, however, were sunken and framed by dark circles, revealing an unmistakable sadness. Although the girl in the portrait was smiling, Annie knew the girl was worried and hiding secrets.

As she flipped through the pages of the book, she realized that all the photos had been taken by her own camera. She pressed the bridge of her nose between her fingers and squeezed her eyes shut, wondering where the pictures Johan had taken were. Then she pressed both hands over the length of her face, covering her eyes and cheeks at the same time, and shook her head. She had no idea what he had photographed and now felt she needed to know.

Annie placed the book in the box and slid it all back under the bed. As she prepared to get up from the carpeted floor, the yellow phone on the nightstand rang out. For a moment, she was stunned and stopped in mid action. Its tone sounded foreign, and she looked at it as it rang a second time. She wasn't sure if she should answer it or let someone else in the house pick up the call. Then the old habit returned, and she picked up the receiver, "Hello?"

"Annie?" A male voice on the other line slurred her name.

"This is Annie. Who is this?" She held her breath because the voice sounded somewhat familiar.

"Um, Uh. It's Jo. Johan." The voice turned breathy.

"Johan, what do you want? You're supposed to be on spring break."

"Yeah. I'm gonna go. We don't leave until tomorrow. Get off my back."

Annie frowned at his tone and choice of words. "What do you want, Johan? You're supposed to be leaving me alone."

"I just want to talk to you. Can't a guy talk to his girf. . . firf. . . girlfriend?"

"Now is not the time to talk. You need to just leave me alone."

"No . . . ooo. I . . . uh . . um . . . have to talk to you. Beef, beefore I go. I want to say I'm shorry . . . I'm . . . sorry."

She imagined he was swaying and holding on to the wall as he spoke. She held her hand over her mouth and didn't respond to his apology. She felt that any comment she made was not going to be heard. She picked up the base of the telephone and moved it to her bed. Then she sat beside it waiting for anything else he had to say.

"You list . . . listen to me," he hiccupped. "You're mine and that's it. You don't get to tell me what to do." He paused and sniffled. "I tell you what to do, you bitch."

"What did you call me?" Annie gasped and stood up by her bed. She pressed her lips together and fought back an urge to yell.

"You heard me."

"Johan, no. We're not speaking anymore."

"You think you're so good. Wait . . . yeah, you're good . . . but you're mine. You're not gonna leave me . . . you little bitch. You're my bitch."

Annie glared at the phone then closed her eyes. She couldn't believe what he was saying, and she didn't want to hear anymore. Anger was starting to percolate inside her. It bubbled up and burned hot in her chest, causing her lungs to work extra hard to control it. She felt the heat move to her ears as she swayed from one foot to the other trying to calm herself. Raising her head and elongating her neck, she pulled her shoulders back and stood tall. Tears that were lining up at the floodgates were pressed back. She couldn't allow herself to cry at that moment.

Somewhere far away in her head, she heard her own voice whispering *Not now, Annie. Don't cry now. He is never going to change, and you can't change him. You deserve more than this.* Annie took a deep breath and nodded in agreement. In one swift move, she gently pressed the receiver button and hung up the phone.

The anger in her chest was pulsating, but her thoughts were distant. She was disconnected from the rage inside her and saw herself moving like one having an out-of-body experience. Her body parts did things without her conscious awareness and took over. They pulled her small brown purse out of her backpack and slung it over her left shoulder. Her legs walked her to the living room, and her eyes and ears noticed that familiar sights and sounds were strange, surreal. Colors were vibrant and outlined, and the TV in the background flowed directly to her. She blinked several times to snap herself out of it and walked into the kitchen. Standing in the doorway, she watched her mother wrap the veal cutlets with cellophane.

Annie felt like she was on the outside looking in, but it was a similar feeling to the time in the dorms when she took a nap at 2:00 pm and woke up at 6:00 pm to Maddie and Christy studying at their desks. For a few minutes, she thought it was the next morning and stressed over everyone having missed class.

Annie's words broke the spell in the kitchen when she asked, "Can I borrow the car for a little while? There's something I need to do."

Without looking up from her work, her mother responded, "Yes. The keys are right there on the table. Be careful."

"I will, Mommy." Annie grabbed the keys and hurried out the back door. She barely settled in the car before she had it in reverse, backed out of the drive, and headed out of the neighborhood toward the fraternity house.

Chapter 24

Against Her

Annie pulled up to the fraternity house and parked on the street. It wasn't difficult for her to gain entrance to the house as the front door was wide open, and fraternity boys were loading two vehicles up with supplies for the beach.

She encountered Luis and Tristan in the living room and slowed down enough to acknowledge them with a little small talk.

"Hello, Annie. Are you going anywhere for spring break?" Tristan asked.

"Yes. I'm going home. How about you?"

"No. I'm staying to work in the dining hall. Luis is staying, too. He doesn't have any money to go anywhere, so I have to feed him."

Luis sheepishly waved at her.

On any other day, Annie would have thought that cute. She looked from one to the other, nodded her head, then bounded up the stairs. In the reflection of the mirror on the first landing of the staircase, she saw Tristan and Luis looking at each other and shrugging their shoulders.

Making it to the top of the stairs, she pushed Johan's bedroom door open and entered while he continued spewing insults at her over the phone. For a second, she thought it funny how he thought she was still at home on the phone line with him. He frowned and his eyes darkened as she stood in the doorway.

"What the hell," he exclaimed as he removed the receiver from his ear, looked at it, looked at her, then slammed it in its cradle. He unsteadily rose from his position on the couch, dropping the whole phone to the floor. "What are you doing here?" The focus in his eyes was off, and his speech was slow and slurred.

Not knowing quite what to do, she stepped cautiously into his bedroom. The sheets were crumpled and bunched up at the foot of the bed. Evidence of the joint he was smoking burned in the amber-colored ashtray resting on the edge of the chipped brown coffee table. A small round mirror, a razorblade, and plastic straw sat haphazardly next to a clear baggie, containing a white powdery substance. She knew what it was and tried not to show her disdain. The hair on the back of her neck rose as she started wondering if she had made a mistake by entering his room.

Contrary to his slurring words, his physical agility was somewhat intact. He stood, and quickly went to his door and locked the three locks.

Annie did not expect this. He now stood between her and the door, and her only other opportunity for escape was to climb out onto the roof through one window or jump out the second window onto the sidewalk below. Both windows were open to their fullest, and the curtains moved gently in the breeze, calling to her, inviting her. Telling her to get out.

Johan, with his six-foot frame and 200 pounds of muscle, rushed her before she could decide on her plan, and he grabbed her by her ponytail. Although unstable while standing on his feet, he showed remarkable strength in his grasp. With one hand, he dragged her around the room, yelling at her.

"You're a bitch! You don't deserve anything good!" he shouted.

Annie screamed, "Let me go! Johan, you're hurting me! Let me go!" She reached for his arm and sank her fingernails into it. Ten polished nails dug in deep and tore his flesh.

"Oh, no you don't!" he roared. Like pulling an overgrown weed from a garden, he shook her by her ponytail to get her to release her nails. It worked. She had to put her hands out to keep from falling, and he got a better hold of her. He bent her over, preventing her from standing up straight, and dragged her around the room. The effects of the drugs he had just consumed made him a bit unsteady on his feet, and he stumbled over the waste basket, spilling its contents across the floor.

"Johan, stop! Someone help! Help me! Johan, stop!" Annie screamed hoping some fraternity boys were still in the house.

On the first floor below, Tristan and Luis heard her screams. They leaped off the couch and bounded up the stairs only to be met by Johan's locked door.

"Tristan, do you have a key?" Luis asked as he pounded on the door.

"No. He said he was going to give it to me when they were ready to leave. I don't have it. What can we do? We have to get Annie out of there." He hammered the door with the side of his fist.

"Johan, open the door! Open the door! Let Annie go!" Luis hollered.

Tristan continued pounding as other fraternity brothers joined them on the second-floor landing.

"Let's break it down!" Someone yelled.

Three brothers smashed their shoulders against the door, but it wouldn't budge.

Someone asked, "Is he high?"

"Yeah. I saw him partying with Greg. He's pretty wasted. Greg took his coke and left a few minutes ago, so Johan is fried right now."

The boys in the hall took turns trying to bust through the door.

They yelled and pounded.

Someone said, "Hey, can we get in from the roof? We can go through Tristan's room."

"Tristan doesn't have a window that opens to the roof. You would have to go through his window and climb a tree limb to get to the roof. Last week, the tree trimmers removed the branch that connected to the roof." Luis shared. "Someone go down to the garage and see if we have a ladder."

Three boys ran down the stairs and out the front of the house. They lifted the garage door and searched for a ladder.

Luis and Tristan continued pounding on the door.

Inside the bedroom, the struggle continued. Johan flung Annie across the room by her ponytail, and she caught the edge of his dresser with the small of her back. She heard something crack and didn't know if it was her body or something on the solid wood top. She spotted the phone on the floor and lunged to get it, but he was faster than her and reached it first. He yanked it out of the wall and threw it and its long white cord out the open window.

Then he came at her with his hands outstretched. She used the dresser to brace herself and all her might to kick him in the stomach with both her feet. Although her legs were not long, they were powerful, and her 100 pounds was mainly muscle. The forceful blow threw him back, and he slipped on a beer bottle that had rolled out of the trashcan. His body crashed into the nightstand against the wall and slid to the floor.

Annie turned and ran to the door. She unlocked each lock and barely opened it when he was up on his feet again bounding across the room toward her.

She threw the door open and ran into Luis and Tristan who had been pounding on it and yelling Johan's name.

Tristan took Annie by the shoulders and yelled, "Run, Annie! Run! Get out of here!"

Annie heard Luis yelling at Johan, "Get back and sit down!"

She didn't look back. She took the stairs two at a time and bolted out the front door. She hurried past fraternity boys who stopped what they were doing to watch her jump into the station wagon. She sped off, but she didn't know where to go, so she turned the corner and went back to the university. She needed to get herself to a place where she could cry and scream and cry some more.

Adrenaline kept her moving. She parked the car in a space close to the building and quickly walked up the stairs to the entrance of her dorm. Slipping past the front desk staff, she hoped nobody would notice her; she wanted to be invisible. She wished for the elevators to be empty because she couldn't hold it in any longer; she was about to burst.

Once at her dormitory door, she jabbed her key in the lock, rushed in, and engaged the deadbolt. Then she threw herself face down on her bed. Heavy tears saturated her bedspread, and the blood that pumped through her veins filled her face, making it red and itchy. She slid to the floor, grabbed her pillow, and for half an hour, screamed into it, hugged her knees, and rocked her body, an old familiar pattern that helped her when she was a child. The heaving sobs came in huge suffocating waves that quaked through her, coursing through every cell in her body until there was nowhere else to go.

Then like the quick dark storms in the Florida Keys, all the tears stopped, and she stared blankly into space, focusing on nothing as her mind and body became numb. Back and forth her body pitched until the momentum diminished, and the energy that controlled her weakened.

When sobs slowed and turned into small shivers, Annie rose from the floor. She wobbled as she stepped down on the heel of her left shoe and wiggled out of it and did the same to the right. Then she walked, fully clothed, into the shower. Under the stream of warm water, tears started again, but this time they were accompanied by thoughts and words.

It's not you, Annie. It's him. You're in a toxic relationship. When you come back from break, go to the counseling center and find someone to talk to.

With her body drenched and the tears melded into the shower water, it was done. She stood with her palms flat against the shower wall and shook her head. She would have no more. She had endured months of abuse to fix something that could never be mended. She had carried the weight of the responsibility for its failure. But no more. People can't be fixed by the ones they abuse. People like Johan need more help than she knew how to give. His problem was bigger than her, and this was not how she wanted to spend the rest of her life.

As she watched the water swirl and go down the drain, she concocted a plan for her healing, and it did not include him. It was something that had been growing in the back of her mind, but guilt and shame wouldn't allow her access to it. She knew the relationship was over, and no amount of begging or apologizing was going to repair the destruction he caused.

She unbuttoned her blouse and stripped it off her shoulders. Her bra was easy, two hooks and done. Next, she, inch-by-inch, pushed her soaked shorts and underwear down and stepped out of them, leaving them wadded up on the tile floor. Lastly, balancing herself against the shower wall, she peeled off her socks. She felt stripped of all that was ugly, beaten, and dead. She turned the shower knob to cold and endured a freezing blast of water that awakened her, cleansed her, made her pores tighten and her skin feel new. She shut off the water and let it run down her as it dripped from her nose, her hair, her fingertips.

She knew now what she needed to do. She could no longer allow the fear of what he might or might not tell her parents to control her. None of his threats mattered anymore.

Picking up her blouse from the floor, she wrung it out in the shower and hung it on a towel rod. Then she picked up her underwear and did the same. She squeezed and twisted each piece of clothing one at a time and hung them. Working meticulously, she focused only on what she was doing. There were no thoughts moving through her mind. It was blank.

Grabbing her towel from a hook near the shower door, she dried her body, patting it gently. Saving her hair for last, she bent over, letting it fall forward, then wrapped it in the towel. She stepped out into her bedroom and found underwear and socks for the day. Then she pulled a pair of white shorts from her closet and sorted through her tops. She held up a black Stevie Nicks concert T-shirt with the image of white wings attached to a pink heart and white letters across the bottom that read, "Don't Blame it on Me." She smiled, nodded, and spoke to herself, "This is the perfect shirt. I now have wings to fly away from all of this."

Annie took a deep breath and began to dress. Without thinking about it and out of habit, she quickly braided her hair. Then she sat on her bed, slipped on her sneakers, and tied them up without looking. She searched the room for other things she needed to put back in order. Finding nothing else, she picked up her pillow and put it back at the head of the bed and straightened the bedding. Her purse and keys were on the floor, so she picked them up and walked out into the hall, firmly closing the door behind her.

Chapter 25

Opened Door

On her way down the hall, she could hear the elevators moving in the distance. She quickened her pace and pushed the "down" button before her steps had come to a complete stop. Both elevators opened at the same time, but the door on the left hesitated a bit, so she stepped into the right one. Only one person was on it, but she didn't make eye contact nor check to see who it was. She faced the door with her back to the stranger but could see a dull reflection of the person behind her.

It was a boy, looking down and fumbling with his keychain.

When he lifted his head, she recognized the shape of his face. She turned to him, and he spoke first. "Annie? I thought you were gone."

"I thought you were gone."

"I am. Uh . . . I was, but I forgot my wallet, so we had to come back. We were at the gas station up the road when I realized that I didn't have it. Are you getting a late start?"

"No. I came back to . . . take care of something." She smiled, feeling some strength. Deciding that the elevator was not a place to tell horror stories. "I am headed home now. Wait. Why are you coming from above the tenth floor?"

"Oh. I got on and forgot to press the button for the lobby, so I had to ride all the way up then come back down. Eh. It happens. When do you come back to the dorm?"

"Saturday."

"Can I call you?"

"That would be nice." She didn't know what to think. She was getting out of one dead and dreadful relationship, and here someone was looking forward to seeing her.

The elevator stopped on the lobby floor, and she and Derek stepped out together. He held the entry door open for her, and she walked through the threshold feeling a hint of warm and fuzzy.

"I'll probably be back before that. Sometimes we have plans to spend the whole week at Port Aransas, but someone always gets sick, or we run out of money for the hotel and have to camp on the beach. Beach camping is only good for a few days. Some of us are Eagle Scouts and we can take it, but most of us are city slickers. Roughing it for too long is not an option."

Annie tossed her head back and laughed. "Wait. You're an Eagle Scout?"

"Yep. Do you want me to recite the oath?" He grinned and held up his right arm with elbow bent at a right angle and three fingers up at attention.

"This is just great to hear. Someday you'll have to tell me all about your project."

They strolled at a slow pace toward the parking lot and descended the stairs. Neither one seemed to be in a hurry. The lot was spotted by a dozen vehicles. Annie walked to her car and said, "Well. This is me." She unlocked the door, and like a gentleman, Derek opened it for her.

He bowed at the waist then extended his hand for her to take as she took her seat behind the wheel. Annie settled into her car.

"Mine is over there." He pointed to an orange and black Firebird three rows down. "Wave to the guys." He waved to three fraternity brothers who stood outside of the vehicle. They waved back.

Annie laughed and waved to them. "Thank you, Derek. I've got to get going. Have a good time."

With that, he shut her door and jogged over to his buddies. Annie thought she heard him exclaim, "That's her. That's her."

She slowly drove out of the parking lot. With the windows down, she could hear the symphony of the male chicharras as they posed on branches, singing their mating songs. Their rising and falling cadence soothed and reminded her of the warm summer afternoons she and some of her siblings, Daniel, Adrian, and Julia, spent spread out on blankets under the trees as they read library books.

As she neared her house, its details appeared more vivid. The white curtains that billowed in and out of the open windows waved her over, beckoning her to come home. The brown trim around the structure outlined the boundaries of her family and made her feel secure. A smile lit her face, and she felt an urgency to enter the safe haven and begin living again.

She parked the car and got out. A longing for what awaited her, for the happiness and laughter that came with being with her family, moved her forward. She needed this.

Annie kept her promises to her mother and siblings about cooking and watching TV. She knew she was safe from Johan since he was out of town, and she was home. As difficult as it was, she was going to have to deal with this when she returned to school. The next few days were meant for family and nothing else.

Chapter 26

Kodachrome Scissors

The end of spring break came rapidly. It was Saturday morning, and Annie was ready to return to her dorm room. If she got back soon enough, she could have some time to herself with no Julia and no roommates.

Angelita placed Annie's backpack on the floor at Annie's feet, and Julia and Mateo climbed into the wagon. Once in their assigned seats, Angelita behind the wheel, Annie front passenger, and Julia and Mateo in the middle bench seat, Angelita patted Annie's hand and said, "I'm glad you came home, mija."

"Me, too, Mamita," Annie answered.

"Me, too," Julia and Mateo chimed.

Angelita turned on the radio as she backed out of the driveway. Jim Croce's "Bad, Bad Leroy Brown" started up, and they all sang the lyrics at the top of their lungs, saying "shush" every time the word "damn" appeared. Laughter and melody filled the car for the eight-minute drive. Before they knew it, they were in the parking lot.

"Well. Here we are. You take care of yourself." Angelita looked at her daughter.

"I will do my best, Mommy." Annie leaned over and kissed her mother's cheek. Then she turned to the two in the backseat. "Bye, you guys. Behave."

They each leaned forward and gave their big sister a hug over the seat. Then Annie exited the car and walked up the stairs to the dormitory entrance. She turned and waved to them; Julia and Mateo kept waving at her until she could no longer see them.

Annie took a deep breath and braced herself for what might be coming next. She walked toward the front desk to see who was on duty. Helen looked up from her V.C. Andrews novel and waved at her.

Annie walked to the elevators, pushed the button and waited. As she caught her reflection in the cold metallic elevator doors, a thought came to her. She turned on her heels and briskly walked to the cafeteria.

Just as she suspected, Tristan was behind the counter, wearing a white apron and a baseball cap.

She strode to his line, and he presented her with a look of concern.

"Hi, Tristan. Thank you for what you did for me last week."

"Annie, I'm so sorry."

"I'm okay. I'm going to be okay. But I need some help from you."

"Sure. Anything." He took a hand towel from the counter and wiped his hands.

"Is Johan back?"

"No. They all come back tomorrow. What's up?"

"I need to get into Johan's room before he comes back. I need something. If you can help me get it, I promise I will never come back to the fraternity house again."

"I have his key. He left it with me. I get off in 15 minutes. Can you wait that long?"

"Oh. Yeah. I'll go up to my room and put my stuff down. Then I'll come back."

"Can I get you anything to eat?"

"No. Thanks. I'll come eat dinner later." She turned and headed to her dormitory.

At the elevators, she waited for the car to reach the ground level as she chewed the side of her thumb. The door slowly opened, and Derek stepped out, almost running into her.

"Hey. You're back," he exclaimed.

"Hey. You're back."

"Yeah, we got back last night. Rick got sick, and so we just ended the trip. It's okay. We were all running out of money anyway. We barely had enough change for gas." He laughed.

Annie stepped into the elevator. "Well. Maybe I'll see you later."

"Yeah. Sure. We'll plan something for the courts."

"Yes. That would be nice."

"Can I get your number?"

"I'm listed. Look me up." Annie smiled at him as the elevator door closed.

"I will," he said.

Annie hurried off the elevator on the 10th floor. Some students were lingering in the hallway, and she worked past them to get to her room. She unlocked the door, switched on the light, and placed her backpack on her desk. Pulling her meal card and ID out of her purse, she slid them into her back pocket. Then she headed back downstairs to meet Tristan.

The dinner shift took over the serving lines, and Annie found Tristan waiting for her by the door.

"Are you ready to go to the house, and are you sure he's not home or coming home today?" she asked as she led him in the direction of the fraternity house.

"Well. They said Sunday, but sometimes things change. How about we go down there, and you hide behind the neighbor's van. I'll check to see who's home. If the coast is clear, I'll come get you. . . What is it that you need? Maybe I can get it for you," he offered.

"Thanks, but I really must do it myself. I'll stay by the van until you come get me." She noticed Tristan's furrowed brow. "Don't worry. What happened last week is never going to happen again. He and I are finished. I am going to make sure of that."

Tristan sighed as they marched in unison the three blocks down the street. Arriving at the neighbor's maroon van, Annie hid in its shade on the side away from the fraternity house. She watched Tristan enter through the open front door. He was gone for two minutes and then returned to her.

"It's clear. Only Luis is home. He said he hadn't heard from anybody. Let's do this," he urged.

"Yes. Let's be quick," she agreed.

They jogged to the door, through the house, and up the stairs. Tristan unlocked the room and flung open the door. Annie worked quickly. She searched around the coffee table and nightstand. Turning toward his dresser and chest of drawers, she spotted the crooked drawer and remembered he had extracted some pictures from there before. She walked to it and pulled it open. It gave out a loud squeak, and she peered inside.

"Bingo!" she exclaimed. She pulled the contents of the drawer out and spread the pictures on the dresser top. Three photo booth envelopes laid among the pile, each one containing three strips of negatives. She pulled the contents of each envelope out and held the negative to the light. If a strip contained her image, she took it and slipped it in her pocket. As quickly as she could, she went through each negative and each photograph. Anything that had her in it was removed and shoved into her back pocket. Then she scoured his room looking for film canisters and his camera.

"Tristan, help me look for anything that might contain my picture." She waved him into the room as she deepened her search.

Together they looked in his closet, in his drawers, around the furniture, between cushions, between sheets. Annie dropped to her knees and looked under the bed. A black and white Puma tennis shoe box sat just beyond her reach.

"Tristan, I found something, but I can't reach it. Can you get it?" She stayed bent over looking at it, fearing it might disappear if she turned away.

"Yeah. What are we doing this for?" Tristan joined her on the floor and reached for the box.

"I am ending everything with him. I don't trust him. And I want to pull any picture he has of me. He doesn't get to have me in any way."

Tristan nodded as he handed her the box.

She straightened and leaned back on her legs. Holding the box in her lap, she hesitated. "Tristan, do you mind looking away?"

Tristan complied.

Annie pulled the cover off. The box contained two film canisters, a camera, and seven black and white photographs of her asleep. She picked up all seven pictures and slowly shuffled through them. Her dark brown hair was spread across the bed, and she looked peaceful in her party dress. One picture showed her right leg hanging over the side with her panties and pantyhose dangling from the ankle. On the sheet beside her was a stain or water mark; she wasn't sure. She took the pictures and shoved them in her pocket. Then she opened the camera and took out the roll of film. It was partially spent, but she didn't care. She pulled the film out until everything on the negative was exposed. She gathered up the loose film and the two canisters and shoved them in her front pocket.

"I think we're done, Tristan. You can turn around now." Annie replaced the lid on the box and slid it back under the bed.

"What did you do?"

"It's better that you don't know anything. I'm going to leave now. Thanks."

They stood together, and she gave him a hug.

Annie fled the fraternity house with no intention of ever returning. Every emotion she was trying to control while in the room with Tristan flooded forward. The black and white pictures made her feel ugly and dirty. Although she didn't remember her rape, the pictures worked as proof that something horrible happened to her. The guilt and shame that weighed her down everywhere she went, poked at her and twisted her insides.

She ran up the street and across the campus all the way to Jesten Hall. Once at the elevators, she jabbed at the "up" button multiple times to get it to hurry. The left door opened, and her knees shook as she waited for five people to move aside and let her in. Slipping past them, she pushed the 10th floor button and gritted her teeth as the elevator sluggishly made its way up.

Once on her floor, the hall was clear, so she ran to her room and got herself inside. Shutting the door, she leaned her back against it. Her body slid to the floor as the anger inside her manifested into hot tears that ran down her face.

Seething rage made her reach for her hair and pull at her long strands. "I can't be that girl with the beautiful hair anymore. He photographed it then used it as bondage against me."

Annie rose from the floor and marched over to her desk. In the center drawer, she withdrew a pair of red-handled scissors. With rage still leading her, she walked to the bathroom and stood in front of the mirror. She felt around the little shelf next to the sink, found two black hair ties, and fastened her hair into a low ponytail that started at her shoulders. Then she took the second hair tie and tightened it around the middle of her ponytail. Grabbing the first tie with her left hand, she picked up the scissors and began to cut directly above it. It took effort as the scissors gnawed at her hair. She felt like they were cutting only one strand at a time. She had to work at it and work at it. She cut and cut until she held what looked like a horse's tail in her hand.

She walked to her desk and dropped the tail in the trash. Then she pulled out all the contents from her pockets and laid them on the desk. Sitting in her chair, she took each picture and began to cut. First, she cut him out of each photograph and then cut across his face. She cut his smile, his eyes, his throat. Then she took her image in every photo and kissed herself goodbye, sliding all the pieces into the trash. Finally, she worked on the negatives. She cut each small tile in every angle. She picked up the trash can and swept everything into its gullet. But her need to cut was not yet fulfilled, so she took the scissors back to the bathroom.

Standing at the sink, a new Annie reflected back at her. She studied her shoulder length hair, moving her head from side to side. She ran her fingers through it and shook it out. Taking Maggie's blue hand mirror from the bathroom shelf, she observed her profile and then the back of her head. She had not had short hair since she was four years old, but this new look suited her. It was sassy and springy.

Annie then used the slender handle of the mirror to part her hair, pulling a section forward to cut bangs. Then she put the mirror down and grabbed the section with her left hand, pulling it down over her face. With the scissor blades centered at her eyes, she cut straight across. Her new bangs sprung up to meet her eyebrows. Then she gathered her new bangs and snipped at their edges so the cut would not be a perfect line dividing her face.

Annie was amazed at the transformation. Her short hair made her face come alive. She felt lighter, stronger, capable of anything. She let the rage subside into anger, the kind one needs to get through a tough ordeal. Then she wadded up several sheets of toilet paper, moistened them with a few drops from the sink, and gathered up the strips of hair that laid like fallen soldiers against the white porcelain, casualties after a war.

As she straightened the bathroom, she felt worry and fear slipping away from her. It felt like the thick rope that once choked her was slowly loosening until she was free from it. He was never going to have a hold on her again. She would stay away, never be in a situation where she was alone with him. There was nothing to patch up - no relationship that needed fixing.

She now had a plan for herself. She would find a good therapist at the counseling center who could help her keep her promises to herself.

Hope was on the horizon.

Chapter 27

Sunday Morning

In the quietness of her dorm room, Annie lay under her blanket and sheets, waiting for the clock to signal the time to get up and eat breakfast. She had not eaten since her mother's breakfast on Saturday, and she was starving. She rolled to her side and watched the time move to 9:00 am.

It was strange to not have her long hair follow her every move. She had never noticed before how her ponytail always dictated how she moved, laid in bed, sat in a chair. She sat up on the edge of her bed and swung her hair from side to side. She even felt a lightness in her neck and back.

Going about her bathroom routine, she brushed her teeth and applied her deodorant. Next, she put on her undergarments and was surprised when she didn't have to pull long hair stands out of her underwear. Then she brushed her hair and swept her bangs to the left. From the closet, she pulled a pair of orange shorts and an orange and white striped tank top from her shelf, an outfit that hadn't been worn in a while. The top easily pulled over her head, no long strands to move out of the way. She finished dressing and was in the middle of tying her shoes when the phone rang.

She looked at the phone and let it ring a second time. "It can be anybody," she said. With a deep breath, she braced herself and picked up on the third ring.

"Hello?" She stood at her desk and held the back of her chair. She wasn't ready to hear Johan's voice.

"Hello, Annie?" came a male voice.

"This is Annie."

"Annie, this is Derek."

Annie let out a sigh of relief as a smile warmed her face. "Hi, Derek. You found my number." *He sounds different on the phone, kinder.*

"Yeah. I hope you haven't eaten, yet. Would you like to go to breakfast?"

"That would be nice." She thought to herself, *That would be nice. That would be nice? Can't I think of something else to say?*

"I think it would be nice, too. How about I meet you in the lobby in ten minutes. Or would ten minutes be long enough?"

"Yes. I was actually headed that way. I'll meet you there."

"Okay. Let's see who gets there first."

"You're on!" She hung up the phone and searched around her room for her things. Keys, check. ID, check. Meal ticket, check. Positive attitude, double check.

Annie ran out the door and down the hall. She pressed the button and rocked on her heels as she waited. As soon as the left door opened, she rushed in and pushed the "close door" button. The car slowly puttered down and stopped at the 8th floor to pick up two people then the 6th floor for three people. Next, it stopped at the 5th floor. As the elevator door opened, she heard the door from the right elevator closing and slowly starting its descent. She tried to pretend she wasn't eager to see who was getting on. This time it picked up two girls and one guy. Derek was not one of them. The elevator's next stop was the second floor, picking up one more hitchhiker. Finally, at the end of the race, the door opened, and all those who got on after her exited first. She was the last one to step out into the lobby, and Derek stood there with a big grin on his face. *Oh, that grin*, she thought.

"Well, hey. I hardly recognized you. That's a great look on you." His eyes lit up and his grin turned to a genuine smile.

"Do you like it?" She touched her hair with the palm of her right hand and batted her eyes.

"I do. I do indeed, Annie. And by the way, I won," he exclaimed.

"Well. You had a head start."

"You might think that, but I waited a few minutes before I got on. See the problem is you got on the left elevator, the slow one." He laughed and said, "Shall we?"

"We shall." She giggled and stepped beside him.

Together they walked to the dining hall and separated when it came to the serving lines. Derek chose the high protein lane, and Annie wanted warm and mushy. The lines were short, so they quickly reunited and found a table in a sunny patch of light next to the windows. It seemed to be lit up just for them.

Derek set his tray on the table and pulled Annie's chair out for her. Then he stood next to his chair and waited for her to take her seat.

Realizing that this had never been done for her before, she stood at her chair, tilted her head, and smiled at him. "Thank you."

"Of, course. Would you expect anything less?"

"Actually, you surprise me every time. You're something else." She smiled and took her seat.

Before her was a large tan bowl filled with oatmeal, raisins, honey, nuts, and cinnamon. As she took her spoon and prepared to stir it, she glanced across the table and found Derek clasping his hands in prayer. She immediately put her spoon down and joined him in a moment of silence. *Yikes. Well, he keeps me on my toes.*

"Alright. Let's dig in."

"Al Ataque!"

Derek laughed. "What did you say?"

"It's what my father always said when we were ready to eat. Attack!" She laughed with him.

"Well. I've got a lot to learn."

Annie began eating, but in her mind, she was grinning from ear to ear. Derek always surprised her with his kind gestures, his supportive words, his good sense of humor. For a fleeting moment she wondered if this was all genuine. Could he really be as nice as he seemed? None of this had ever been shown to her by any boy she had dated before.

Then the butterflies in her stomach returned. They flitted about haphazardly with no sense of rhythm. She shook her leg under the table to make them stop because they were getting distracting. But the truth was that she hadn't known happiness in a long time and had forgotten it. She hadn't felt special in a long time, but Derek was bringing that back.

She decided not to question it for the moment and just to enjoy their Sunday with good company and nutrition.

Derek sat across the table, gathering his utensils and napkin as positive thoughts about her flooded forward. He hoped she wasn't a mind reader, or he'd have to explain himself. As the sun streamed between them, it caught the gleam in Annie's eyes and lit her face. He had never noticed the tiny freckles across her nose before. He admired this beautiful young woman who sat before him. She was smart, witty, and kind. But more than this, he viewed her as strong. She possessed an inner strength that he had never known a girl to have. He had dated several girls, but they were nothing compared to Annie. He wasn't even sure if he was good enough for her, but he would wait and remain her friend.

After he finished his last piece of bacon, he gulped down his orange juice and wiped his mouth with his napkin. She was still working on her oatmeal, so he waited for her to take her last spoonful and drink of water.

"Are you done?" he asked.

"I am. I think I need to go take a little nap," she confessed.

"That's not a bad idea. Oh. I forgot to ask. Do you think you want to hit the courts sometime this week?" He hoped she would say yes.

"That's a great idea. Let's see what kind of homework we're given. Dr. Braidwood usually sticks to his syllabus, but sometimes he throws a twist. It really depends on how people are answering his questions and participating in Socratic seminars. Otherwise, I'm wide-open Friday afternoon and all day Saturday. Oh, and by the way, I still have your towel."

He liked how she talked with her hands when she described something she was interested in. "Okay then. I'll call you Wednesday evening. Maybe by then we'll know if Thursday is open, too."

When breakfast was over, he let her take her own tray to the bin. He didn't want her to feel that he thought she couldn't do anything for herself. She certainly was an independent woman, and he wanted to respect that.

They exited the dining hall and walked into their tower still talking about tennis, the weather, upcoming social events. Derek just liked to hear her talk. The right elevator door opened and ten people spilled out and headed to the dining hall. Annie stepped in, and Derek followed. For some reason, the ride to the fifth floor seemed much shorter than usual.

"Well. This is my stop. I'll see you later." The doors opened, and he stepped out, turned to her, and pretended to tip an invisible hat on his head.

"See you later." She waved as the doors closed.

Chapter 28

Pathetic Apology

After breakfast, Annie returned to her room and stuffed her keys in her pocket. Then she pulled her dried garments from the towel racks where she had left them the week before. They were a bit stiff, so she laid them on her bed, smoothed them out with the palms of her hands, then hung them up in the closet.

She walked over to her trashcan and pulled out the liner containing all her cuttings from the day before. Tying the top end of the bag into a knot, she took it to the trash shoot at the end of the hall away from the elevators and disposed of them. It was done. That part of her was both literally and symbolically gone.

As she returned to her room, she heard the phone ringing and hurried in. Picking up on the fourth ring this time she said, "Hello?"

"Hello, Annie. It's me, Johan." His somber, sober voice did nothing for her.

"What do you want?"

"I want to talk to you. I'm sorry. I'm sorry for everything I did and everything I said. I love you, Annie. I don't want to lose you." His groveling disgusted her.

"No. I don't believe you. You are one sorry, pathetic person, a poor excuse of a man. There is no love between us. There hasn't been in quite a while. We're done. Finished. Never to be again. I don't care what you threaten, but I have witnesses to what you did to me last week, and I have witnesses to what you did to my car. And my mom knows how you treated me that night I got out of the car and had to get away from you. It's over. You hear me? And if you know what's good for you, you better just stay away. I have five brothers and a protective father who wouldn't stop beating the shit out of you. You're no prize." All the words that she always wanted to say to him just came spewing out.

***

Johan sat in a chair on the second floor of the fraternity house. He was having to use the community phone as the phone jack in his bedroom was destroyed, and the phone he had thrown out the window was broken into pieces from having hit the sidewalk.

The words that Annie spoke stung him, yet he knew she was right. There was no coming back from this.

"Okay. I'll stay away. I won't bother you ever again."

"We're done. And if you ever come near me again, YOU will pay the price this time." With those final words, the phone call ended. Her tone, her words, her threat rang loudly in his ears.

Johan hung up the receiver and went into his room. He sat on his couch and looked around at the destruction. Whatever happened here was bad, but he really had no memory of it.

Chapter 29

Turned Corner

The long shadows of Sunday evening painted their charcoal silhouettes of the Venetian blinds along the wall across from Annie's bed. She lay on her back with her head on her pillow, hands behind her head, legs crossed at the ankles, waiting for Maddie and Christy to return.

Thoughts about how she planned to make that call to set up her therapy sessions at the counseling center filled her head, and she wished that she had done so earlier. In a split second, she started blaming herself for the delay that could have prevented some of the things that happened to her. Then she shook her head. "No. I'm not going to blame myself for this anymore. This relationship was over months ago, and now I'm proud of myself because I'm here, and I'm safe."

At 4:30, a key turned in the lock, and Maddie entered with a small suitcase. "Hello. I'm home," she sang out.

"You are." Annie rose to greet her.

"Oh, Annie. You look adorable!" Maddie hugged her. "This is great. When? Where did you get it done?" She gently touched Annie's hair.

"Yesterday. And I did it. It was time."

"Time?" Maddie shook her head, not quite understanding.

"I'll explain when Christy gets in so I only have to tell it once. Any idea when she might be getting here?" Annie sat on her bed.

"Actually, she's downstairs. I was already entering the building when I saw her car pulling in. I couldn't wait for her because I had to go to the bathroom. Excuse me. I'll be right back." Maddie rushed into the bathroom and shut the door.

Annie lay back on her bed and returned to watching the shadows grow.

A key in the lock turned and Christy entered with her small suitcase and her backpack.

"Hey, Annie. It's so good to see you."

"Hey, Christy." Annie sat up in the bed and waited for Christy to put the luggage down.

Christy turned to face Annie.

"Surprise," Annie whispered.

"What? I . . . wow. You look fabulous. I am surprised," Christy stretched her arms out to hug her. "What made you decide to cut your hair?"

"It's a long story, and I want to tell the two of you at the same time."

"Okay."

Maddie entered the room and hugged Christy. "So glad you're back."

"I'm glad to see both of you," Christy said.

Annie took control of the conversation and said, "First, let's go to mass then to dinner. After that we can tell all our stories."

The three girls gathered their purses and left the dorm room. Maddie hummed the melody to "They Will Know We are Christians by Our Love" as they walked down the hallway, and Christy and Annie joined in with a little harmony. Elevator door B opened, and they stepped in.

The song continued as they moved one floor at time down the elevator shaft, stopping on the eighth to let in two people. The newcomers smiled and joined in on the humming. When they reached the fifth floor, Annie found it difficult to continue her part in the harmony because her breath kept catching in anticipation of who might be getting on. The door opened and Derek entered. Annie looked at her hands, trying to hide her interest.

Derek looked around the small crowd of hummers and joined in. Soon the whole song played out as they rode down to the lobby floor.

On the walk to church, a warm breeze started and shook the leaves in the trees against each other, making whispering sounds up and down the street. The group turned the corner as they chattered about how much they needed the break from their studies.

Derek pulled the door open and allowed his group to pass. Once inside, he pulled Annie aside and asked, "Are you okay if I sit with you today? I usually sit with my brothers, but we have been together all week."

"Oh, yes. That will be fine. We like sitting near the back." She took the holy water, blessed herself, and followed Maddie to the third to last row on the right side.

Then she genuflected and entered into the pew. Derek followed her.

They sat for an hour next to each other, and Annie felt at peace, something she hadn't felt in public in a long time.

She liked how Derek prayed aloud, how he sang the hymns, and how he wasn't afraid to show his faith.

***

Derek tried to listen to the liturgy, but he felt a bit distracted. Annie, sitting beside him, just seemed right. Something about her was sweet and angelic, and another side seemed mysterious. He had not been able to stop thinking about her since he saw her with her sorority sisters in the dining hall weeks ago. She filled his mind more every time they had a chance encounter, at the tennis courts, on the elevator, in the lobby. He decided he would ask her tonight if she was seeing someone. He thought, *What's the worst that can happen? She says she's involved with someone? She says she's not interested? She says she's a lesbian?*

In his personal intentions, he prayed that God guide him to the right person for him. If it was not Annie, then perhaps someone good would come into his life.

Before he knew it, the time for communion began. That meant that mass was almost over, and he was going to have to face his fear and ask her. He rose from his kneeling position in the pew, placed the kneeler in the up position, and stepped out in the aisle. Annie followed him, and Christy and Maddie were close behind. They walked in reverence to the altar, and Derek received the eucharist. As he pulled off to the side to make the sign of the cross, he caught a glimpse of Annie at the altar with her arms crossed against her chest, a sign that she felt she was not in a state of grace. Derek wondered why but immediately dismissed it as none of his business. That was between her and God.

At the end of mass, the congregation slowly moved out onto the sidewalk. Chatter began once the bells rang out. Laughter and hugs spread throughout the small crowd of worshiping students, and Derek felt content.

Derek saw the three girls moving out of the crowd and heading toward him. He smiled and offered both his arms to anyone who would take them. Maddie took his left arm and Christy took his right. Annie led the group back around the corner and up the street to school.

Chapter 30

No Secrets

After everyone was seated for dinner, Christy led the dinner blessing. Then everyone dug in. The banter between the four was light and playful. There was love flowing through the group, and Annie felt safe.

After Maddie and Christy finished their meals, they excused themselves from the table, took their trays to the tray return bin, and left the dining hall.

Derek and Annie sat finishing up the last sips of their sodas.

Derek spoke first. "Annie, can I ask you something?"

"Sure. Shoot."

"Well, I've been wanting to ask you for a while, but there just never seemed to be a good time."

"Okay. Is now a good time?"

"Yeah. I think it is. Okay. . . Umm . . . Are you seeing anyone?"

Annie rang her fingers through her wavy brown hair, smiled, and said, "No. Definitely not."

"Oh. Good." Derek let out an audible exhale.

"But I do have to tell you that I was dating someone, but it really ended in December. I had just been trying to fix the relationship, thinking that I had to. But it's over. I ended everything before break, but like I said, it was over in December."

Derek sat back in his chair and looked into Annie's chocolate brown eyes. He nodded his head and said, "Good."

Annie continued, "I'm going to start counseling for support, but I'm not ready to start anything romantic with anyone right now. I'd like to spend some time working on myself. I feel that if I can strengthen myself, then I can give selflessly to someone else who deserves it. Does that make sense?" She lightly bit the inside of her lower lip, hoping she didn't scare him away.

"I can respect that. I think that's great." He nodded and smiled at her.

"Derek, I like our friendship. I think you are a really sweet person and such a gentleman. I would like to play tennis with you again and see you at church. Is that something we can do?" She looked at him and gave him a small smile.

He responded with a grin. "Tennis buddies? You bet. And church - well that's a given."

They both laughed, and Annie felt respected. The butterflies in her stomach took up line dancing right then and there.

"Well." Derek looked at his watch. "We've got class tomorrow. Can I walk you to your floor? Well, I mean, can I ride up the elevator to your floor?"

Annie found him charming and noticed a little sweat mustache forming on his upper lip.

"Yes. I would like that very much. Are you ready?" She rose and pushed in her chair. With her tray in her left hand, she reached for her little purse and slung it over her shoulder.

Derek rose, scooted his chair in, and picked up his tray. They walked to the tray return bin together and discarded their trash.

As they sauntered toward the exit door, Annie looked out the row of windows on the right of the room and spotted Johan walking up the sidewalk. Alone. He looked small and deplorable. She had no room in her heart or mind for him.

She took a deep breath and turned her focus to walking calmly out the door. She and Derek walked toward the elevators, and he pressed the "up" button. Elevator A arrived, and Derek allowed Annie to step in first. They rode up to the tenth floor, and the elevator door dinged. Annie stepped out as Derek held the door open by blocking the sensor with his body.

"Well. This is where we part. Have a good night and good luck with your classes tomorrow. Maybe we can meet for breakfast, sometime." He grinned.

"I'd like that. Thanks. Have a good night." She waved to him then turned toward the security door that led to her hall. Swiping her ID card, she heard the locking mechanism click, and she turned toward the elevator. She watched as the door slowly closed with Derek inside still looking at her.

Annie giggled then led herself down the hall.

Before unlocking the dorm door, Annie took a deep breath and prepared herself for what she had to do next.

She needed to tell her sisters what she had been going through. She put the key in the lock, turned it, and stepped onto another page in her story.

She didn't hesitate and started right away. "Girls. I want to let you know that I secretly saw Johan. It was not because I loved him. Because I didn't. It was because I didn't know that I was worth anything else. He said and did some horrible things to me over these past several months, and somehow, I found the strength to get away from him. No one will ever treat me like that again. Ever. Going home during break helped me remember what love really is."

Maddie and Christy both sat on their beds, their eyes blinking, their mouths not saying a word.

"I'm not ready to say out loud all that I have been through. I am not ready to describe anything in detail. But I can say that it was bad. And I am grateful that somewhere inside me, I had the strength to end it. It's over." Annie walked across the room and sat in her desk chair as she waited for someone to say something. Time tiptoed about the room, but she could hear its tiny march coming from the watch on the shelf next to her head, its cogs ticking and clicking. She stared at a white piece of paper, the kind that falls off when you rip a sheet out of a spiral notebook, on the dark carpet. Then she looked at Maddie who had her purple spiral opened to a blank sheet.

Maddie rose and moved to Annie. She bent over and kissed her on the check, then hugged her. No words were spoken.

Christy walked over to Annie and hugged her. Annie hugged her back then sat on the floor.

The three girls sat on the floor, legs stretched out, backs resting against their beds. Christy nodded and smiled. Maddie nodded, too.

Annie spoke first. "All of this is a part of me. Everything I've been through, the two of you here with me, my family who loves me."

"Yes," Christy interjected. "All of it."

Maddie, with her way of turning a serious moment into something funny, turned to Christy and chirped, "And now Derek has a part, too."

Annie laughed, reached back and grabbed her pillow and hurled it at her. Maddie caught it, threw it back, and grabbed her own. Before they knew it the girls were in an all out pillow fight until Annie yelled, "Kings! Kings!"

"What the heck does that mean?" Maddie snorted.

"It means I surrender," Christy yelled.

"Surrender? Never!" Maddie continued until everyone settled down and returned to their beds.

"Well. Did anything good happen for anyone this week?" Annie pumped.

"I slept in a lot," Maddie admitted.

"I got some new floppy disks. And you?" Christy inquired.

"I got to spend time with Julia, Mateo, and Mom. My dad was on the road. The others are out on their own. I didn't expect to see them. And . . . well . . . I ran into Derek several times."

"What? I knew it!" Maddie squealed. "I just see a spark there. I see one every time."

"Well, are you interested?" Christy looked directly at Annie.

"Hm. I really can't say. I must do things for myself first. But I can tell you that he is very sweet, and we have a lot of things in common. I think for now I just want to be friends."

Christy reclined on her side, bent her elbow, and propped her head up with her hand. "You're setting boundaries, and that's a good plan if I've ever heard one."

Annie smiled, rose from her bed, and retrieved her pajamas. She stepped into the bathroom, the scene of the slaughter and then the rebirth, and dressed for the night. When she returned, her sisters were already tucked into their beds.

She walked to the door and turned off the lights. The room was transformed into a place of slumber, at least for the next six hours. She shuffled her way through the dark to her bed and slipped in between the sheets. Within minutes her eyelids had become heavy, and her mind started to drift.

Maddie whispered, "Good night."

Christy yawned and whispered back, "Good night."

Annie hesitated in her drowsiness then found the voice to coo, "Sweet dreams."

Epilogue

Fifteen Years Later

Derek looked up the aisle as his knees knocked together. The altar behind him was softly illuminated by candles and a few recessed lights. The room was a bit chilly, but his coat and tie kept him warm. The comforting scent of frankincense, an all too familiar smell, permeated the room. It brought back memories of his days of altar serving and the first time he was the thurifer and responsible for the thurible, the metal bowl that carried the incense. He didn't know what happened. He was swinging it by the chain like he was taught by Father Bob, and before he knew it, he was faced down on the burgundy carpet, charcoal and incense burning little black holes in the worn path. The deacon took a little gold spoon from his pocket, scooped the burning pieces up from the floor, and placed them back where they belonged. Derek was so embarrassed.

Now, here he stood, headed to an experience he wasn't sure he was ready for. He was so nervous and not certain if he knew how to maneuver it. No one had ever taught him, and there were no "how to" books in the library. He checked. A part of him consoled him with the fact that it's a part of life, and most people experienced it. Yet, nothing prepared him for how much his body would shake and how fast his heart would beat in his chest.

One thing he knew for sure was he loved the woman at the end of the aisle. He loved her with all his heart. He met her during a very dark time in her life, and still, he found her worthy. Their friendship blossomed into something magnificent, and now here they were, companions for life. He was confident that she loved him, too.

Derek's mental wandering was halted when he spotted Annie's family gathering at the back of church. All her brothers were dressed in coats and ties, and even Julia wore a dress.

The march began, and everyone stood. All heads were turned to the entrance. Derek could see the pews filled with aunts and uncles, cousins, friends. He saw his own mother and father several rows beyond him. His mother smiled at him before she turned away. He saw the wet glisten in her eyes; she had been crying. He wanted to rush to her and hug her.

Lifting his eyes to see beyond the pews, beyond the people, he spotted her, his Annie. He hadn't seen her in a few days as she was busy working on the ceremony and taking care of the finishing touches. But there she stood at the entrance to the church. Beautiful, radiant. Her father was at her side and her sister on her other side. Annie wore a dark purple dress, her favorite color, and a small black veil over her head. The priest led the procession with incense that perfumed the room. Her family filed in behind the pearlized lavender casket. Annie's face was streaked with tears and the tip of her nose was red. She held a blue tissue in one hand, and a large white magnolia in the other, her mother's favorite flower.

Derek held the hands of their two youngest children while the two older ones held his arms. He looked down at the tops of their heads and realized that this was the saddest moment in their lives, too.

Angelita was gone. She was the glue that kept the whole Cisneros family together, and now she was gone. He didn't know the depth of this kind of sadness, and at the same time, he could remove himself from some of it because his own parents were still living. These were thoughts he would never share with anyone.

Derek turned forward with the crowd as the ceremony began. He hoped he could be strong enough for her, to walk beside her in her grief. This was something he didn't know how to do. He doubted his skills, but he wouldn't ever show her that.

The last time they stood at this altar together, he had made a promise to her through their vows. He took them seriously. Now here they were at the first "worse" of their married life. He resolved that they would move together through it. This grief was now a part of her, too.

***

Annie endured verbal, emotional, and physical abuse from her boyfriend and struggled through it by herself because she did not know enough about abuse to recognize the signs, thinking that all relationships were turbulent. She wished that she had sought help sooner and reported her abuser to the authorities so he could have received the appropriate consequences and not hurt anyone else.

If you or someone you care about is experiencing domestic violence, in a toxic relationship, or struggling with the effects of abuse, reach out for help.

:: 255 ::

National Domestic Violence Hotline
1-800-799-7233

About the Author

Patty Spence is a native of San Antonio, Texas. She received a Bachelor's in Psychology at Saint Mary's University followed by a Master's from Corpus Christi State University (Texas A and M University Corpus Christi). She is a licensed professional counselor with 38 years of experience in the mental health field and recently retired, after teaching American Literature for 21 years. She has three grown children, and as an empty-nester, resides on the bay's edge of Corpus Christi, Texas, with her husband.

Other Books by P. A. Spence

ADULT

Beneath the Sweet Magnolias

Paperback, Kindle

CHILDREN

The Many Adventures of Kiki the Flying Squirrel

Paperback, Kindle, Audio

The Many Adventures of Domino the Common Raccoon

Paperback, Kindle

www.ingramcontent.com/pod-product-compliance
Lightning Source LLC
Chambersburg PA
CBHW061152210726
48294CB00006B/1651